STRAIN

CLARY INGRAM

REAL WORLD
PUBLICATIONS

Copyright © 2012 Clary Ingram
All rights reserved.
ISBN-10 0615572332
EAN-13 9780615572338
Library of Congress number: 2011963023
Real World Publications

A special thanks to all of my supporters.

Clary Ingram

1

AFTER SCHOOL, I FOLLOWED DOUG into the convenience store. My homie chased down his mule like a madman. Pablo owed him two hundred bucks for an ounce of marijuana. We cut through each aisle until we had him cornered. I stood in the cut while Doug stepped to him.

"Where's my money?" he said.

"I don't have it today," Pablo stuttered.

Doug looked down and noticed the pair of Jordans on his feet; the brand-new ones that came out this month for $170. "Don't play wit' me. Give me my money, chico!"

Pablo was trembling. "I don't have it."

Doug bit down on his bottom lip. "I should kick yo' ass. Give me those shoes."

Pablo quickly took off his shoes and handed them to Doug. Then he promised Doug he'd have his package tomorrow.

"You better have my money tomorrow or it's a wrap!" he said, making a throat-slashing gesture. A second later, Doug started grabbing food off the shelves and stuffing them inside his pockets. Our attention shifted to Abdullah, who was standing behind the register.

"No way José. You boys know the rules: one customer at a time in my store!" he said, pointing us towards the door.

Doug gave me the eye and I headed out of the store. Abdullah was hip to the game, although at times, he'd get robbed blind.

I stood outside dribbling the rock as I waited on Doug. A hefty crowd started to circle in front of the store. After school, Abdullah's Food & Gas Mart was the hangout spot while some students waited on their rides.

My homie, Six-Nine, rolled up to a gas pump in his Toyota Corolla. He and I were teammates on the basketball squad. The cat had a mean post-up game. A couple of college recruiters were on his jock after he put up big numbers at last summer's AAU tournament. I on the other hand had to sit out due to a foot injury I'd suffered at the beginning of last season.

Six-Nine got out and started pumping his gas. "What's up, J? You coming out to the park to ball with us?" he said.

"Nah, I'm trying to take it easy, bro. I can't afford to take any chances."

"You can't let one injury affect your mind frame."

"I'm good, you go 'head."

"You sure?"

I looked down at my foot. "I'm positive."

He stopped the pump at five dollars and then hopped in his car. "Alright, I'll catch you later."

"Deuces."

After a few minutes, Doug ran out of the store. Abdullah came to the door with his fist raised high yelling at the top of his lungs, "I'm calling the cops!"

I took off, too, and caught up with Doug halfway down the block. The sun was beating down on us. I wiped the sweat from my forehead as we bent over to catch our breath. I was dying for some ice-cold water. After we caught a breather, we headed up the block. Doug handed me a honey bun and it hit the spot.

"Yo, you should've got us something to drink too," I said, licking the glaze off my fingertips.

Doug and I were homies, but we were complete opposites. He would do sneaky crap that I couldn't see myself doing like stealing, selling weed, and causing trouble. Doug stood about five eight, but he had the heart of a seven-foot giant. Looking at his albino skin and grey eyes, no one would've ever suspected a monster. I tended to take the blame because I was bigger and blacker. At 6'4", I was a spitting image of my pops; I had his chiseled face, sharp nose, and chocolate-brown skin.

Me and Doug lived on the same block in Liberty City – a block filled with small candy-colored houses, but it was no theme park. Outside our windows, there was no green grass or happy children playing in the streets. The drug dealers, thieves, and prostitutes made it a nightmare on 63rd Street. There were times we'd witness drug deals that had gone sour. I hated watching lifeless bodies drop to the pavement at the instant pull of a trigger. I hated bumping into crack heads and prostitutes who would beg to turn tricks in exchange for cash. My block was like a horror movie without an end.

As Doug and I headed up the block, a 550 Benz with shiny rims rolled past us. Louie was pushing the whip. He was a bronze-skinned, curly-haired, Dominican dude with more tattoos than a tattoo shop. His name was well known on the streets. He made fast money and his family owned a couple of businesses.

Doug pounded a fist into the palm of his hand. "Dayum, that's a fresh-ass Benz! Do you know how many girls would spread 'em, if that were us?" he said, bouncing on his tiptoes excitedly.

"Calm down, bro," I said. Girls were the last thing on my mind. Basketball was my focus of attention because it was fun. It also kept me busy and out of trouble. During the summers, I attended basketball camp, while my homies ran the streets and hustled on street corners. My mother was my biggest supporter because she feared losing me to the violence that plagued the streets of Liberty City.

As Doug ran his mouth, I started weaving the rock between my legs. The sound of my basketball pounding the pavement was like sweet music to my ears. I was in another world while Doug named a list of girls he'd smash if he were paid. Meanwhile, I imagined leading my team to a state championship and sinking the winning shot. A smile spread across my face as I envisioned holding the trophy; the thought of it gave me goose bumps. Every day I dreamed of doing things that seemed impossible, like earning a free ride to college on a basketball scholarship.

"Did you hear me?" Doug said.

"What did you say?"

"Nothing, never mind. I hate how you ignore me, dawg. It's like you live out in space."

* * *

"Jermaine, get up, boy! You're going to be late for school," Momma yelled.

"I'm up!" I got out of bed, dreading a long boring day of school. After I laid out my clothes, I headed to the bathroom in the hallway. Coincidentally, Roy was standing in the hallway buttoning his shirt. We brushed shoulders as I squeezed past him.

"Would it kill you to say good morning?" he said, eyeing me.

"Morning."

"When's your first game, son?"

"Why?"

"I would like to be there to show my support if you don't mind."

I walked into the bathroom. "That's alright, I'm good, bro," I said, closing the door in his face. Roy was my stepfather. He and I used to be cool until one night I caught him cheating on my mother. I found him and a woman smashing in his Cadillac Deville. Momma was six months pregnant at the time. After I told her, she still didn't drop that zero. At times, I felt my mother didn't have the strength to leave because she had two little girls to raise. I loved my sisters to death, but I hated their old man with a passion. That day I caught him creeping, I lost all respect for him. Immediately, I'd developed a short-term memory for all the good things he'd done for me as a kid. From that point on, I treated him like any other dirt bag off the street. I was hateful because I felt as though Momma deserved the world. She didn't deserve to be mistreated; it was bad enough that Roy wasn't my real father. I felt like my biological father was a real man. He died taking care of

4

his family. My father was an officer killed in the line of duty when I was seven years old. Even though I was too young to remember a lot of things, I remembered him teaching me how to pee and shoot hoops.

After I used the toilet, I started brushing my teeth. In less than two minutes, someone banged on the door. "What?" I said.

"Will you come outta the bathroom, Jermaine? It's a quarter till seven."

"Momma, I just got in here a few minutes ago."

"Open the door!"

I opened the door and Momma was standing there in her Publix uniform. Every morning, she looked good despite her wardrobe. My mother was petite and fair-skinned with short hair.

"All this going to bed late on school nights is going to have to stop. You have twenty minutes to get out the door. You hear me?" she said.

"Yes, ma'am."

Momma held out twenty dollars.

"I don't need it," I said.

She put a hand on her hip. "I beg your pardon?"

"I'ont need it," I mumbled with a mouth full of toothpaste.

"Why don't you need it?"

I rinsed the toothpaste out of my mouth. "I save my money."

Momma looked at me suspiciously. I knew she thought I was scheming because I had crooked friends. Through her eyes, I was guilty by association. Although most of my homies did their dirt, I had my own mind; I wasn't a follower. Some of them committed crimes from A to Z, but I chose to do honest hard work, like wash cars and cut grass.

"Jermaine, let me tell you something –"

"Oh boy, here we go. Momma, I'm gonna be late for school." I grabbed my washcloth out the shower.

"Don't turn your back when I'm talking to you."

"Hold on, I gotta wash my face."

"No, you, hold on."

I gave her my full attention. "Yes, Momma."

"Trouble is easy to get into, but hard to get out of, Jermaine. I've already had to bury your father and I'll be damned if I have to bury a child too. Now take this money before I hurt you, Negro," she said.

I took the money to ease her mind. Even though I was a 17-year-old grown man, Momma treated me as if I was fresh out of her womb. "Thank you," I said, kissing her on the cheek. Then I washed my face.

Momma stood in the doorway watching me pick out my short nappy 'fro. "Child, if you don't look like your father," she said, smiling.

"Okay are you gon' let me do my thing or what?"

She gave me the talk-to-the-hand sign. "You need to hurry up."

I sighed. "Momma, chill."

"Alright, I'll see you later, baby."

After she left, I thought of skipping. Sometimes, Doug and I would skip and chill at the crib. Today I had a bad feeling about staying home; therefore, I threw on my clothes and headed out the door.

I caught the bus to school. My school was considered an F school and labeled a dropout factory. At Miami Northwest High, education wasn't a priority for a lot of students. The lack of education brought on a lot of ignorance and violence. Every day there was a fight going down in the hallways or the parking lot. The girls kept up a lot of trash and most of them were more interested in getting their hair and nails done than getting good grades. Dudes at school possessed the same mentality, except it was all about who had the freshest Js, biggest rims, and loudest bump in the trunk. It was hard not to get caught up in the whirlwind, but I remained focused. My heart was set on balling and getting a scholarship.

After my third block class, Doug dragged me into the bathroom. "What are you doing, bro? I gotta go to class." I hated being late to Mr. Thomas' math class; he liked to shine on people.

Pablo was standing at a stall taking a leak. Doug pushed him. "You got my money, bitch?"

"Uh," he stuttered.

"Don't stutter."

"Come on, Doug, let it go, bro," I said, looking at my watch.

"Hell no, I ain't gon' let it go. This is his third time tryin' me like a sucker. He owes me money and I want my shit!"

"Just come on." I opened the door and walked out of the bathroom. Seconds later, Doug ran out and followed me down the hall. The vice-principal caught us roaming the hallway.

"Why aren't you two in class?" she said.

Doug sucked his teeth. "We on our way."

Mrs. Jones looked at him. "I'll walk you two to class – and pull up your pants, young man."

"I don't have a belt," Doug said, giving her a hard time.

Mrs. Jones let him slide without sending him to I.S. "Have one tomorrow," she said. When I walked into class, Mr. Thomas didn't open his mouth. I sat at my desk, anticipating his class to end. Instead of paying attention, my head was on other things, like lunch and working out. I was too hungry to concentrate on math.

As soon as the bell rang, I hauled ass. I caught a ride to McDonalds with a cute Spanish girl in my class named Carmelita. A bunch of her pretty friends came along, too. We were packed in a Honda Civic like sardines. One of them sat on my lap in a pair of skimpy shorts. It seemed like a long ride, as I fought to keep my hormones under control.

When we got back to school, the police was deep on the scene. A news truck was parked outside of the school too. It was like a horror scene out of a movie. Everyone in the car went into panic mode except for me. Then everybody got out of the car asking questions.

One of my homies on the basketball squad caught up with me. "Yo, did you hear what happened?" he said.

I stuffed the last bit of French fries in my mouth and said, "No."

"Some boy named Pablo got stabbed in the bathroom."

"For real?" My heart started pounding at full speed.

"Yes sir-ree. They say he crawled outta the bathroom bleeding all over the place."

"Aw man."

The bell rung and I hurried up to class. I was hearing all kinds of stories. My conscience was killing me because I knew Doug was the culprit. I couldn't concentrate in class. Usually all my attention would be spent admiring my English teacher who looked like Janet Jackson. Ms. Love roamed the room and stopped at my desk. My book bag was unpacked while my basketball sat on the desk.

"Mr. Jermaine Parker," she said, placing both hands on her curvy hips.

"Yes, ma'am."

"Don't think you're special. Open your book and follow along."

I set my basketball down and put my book on the desk. "What page are we on?"

Everyone started laughing.

My teacher shook her head. "Will somebody be kind and tell Mr. Parker what page we're on?"

One of the chicas in my class said, "Page eighty-four."

"Gracias, señorita." I opened my book and turned to the page.

"You may start reading where we left off," Ms. Love said.

I started reading aloud as she stood over my shoulder. Five minutes later, the school's resource officer stuck his head in the classroom and asked if he could see me.

"Oooooh," everyone shouted.

I grabbed my things and got up, thinking I was in big trouble.

"Please, everyone, get back to work," Ms. Love said, holding open the door for me.

I followed the officer to the principal's office. There were three police officers and the head principal waiting for me. My throat was dry and my palms were sweaty.

"Have a seat, Mr. Parker," my principal said.

At that moment, I visualized sitting inside of a prison cell. My heart started pounding as the questions began.

"We have a stabbing victim by the name of Pablo Vazquez.... Do you know anyone who may've witnessed the incident?" my principal said.

"Nope," I said.

Everyone started drilling me with a bunch of questions, but they couldn't get a word out of me. I slouched down in my chair, seeming cool, calm, and collected.

One of the officers leaned over the desk and looked me in the eye. "I want you to be aware of the criminal charges you could face if you're withholding information from authorities."

"Like I said: I didn't see nothing so can I leave now?"

"You may leave," my principal said, shaking her head.

I walked out of the principal's office and took a deep breath. I wanted to kill Doug.

After school, I headed to the weight room. Doug trailed me upstairs to the weight room as if I needed the headache. I couldn't believe he didn't show any type of pity. The presence of him made me nervous. I didn't want him around me at all.

"Slow down," he said, rushing up the stairwell.

I stopped and looked at him. "Look, bro, I'm trying to stay focused this year. I ain't got time for bullshit."

He stepped close to me. "What you tryin' to say?"

"Do you realize you had me caught up in the middle of your garbage? Both of us could've gone down, bro," I whispered, as people walked past us.

Doug seemed unfazed. "Look at you gettin' all worked up and shit," he said, patting me on the chest.

I brushed his hand away and he started laughing. "You're crazy. Stay away from me," I said, walking into the weight room. I could feel him breathing down my neck.

"Me and you go all the way back, dawg. Let's squash it," he said.

"You wrong, bro."

He put his arm around my neck. "Just relax; he'll be a'ight."

After a hectic day, I focused my energy on a heavy workout. I refused to let anything stop me from achieving my goals. I was about business. The season was approaching and I didn't have time for playing around. Coach had made it clear to me that he expected big things from me. Before my foot injury, I was the second-leading scorer on the squad, averaging 17 points per game. Last year's leading scorer and all-time assists leader, Kevin Smith, had chosen to quit the team and play football. I felt like the world was on my shoulders, because I was used to him playing at the point guard position. My strength was playing off the ball, but Coach wanted me to play point guard.

I had big shoes to fill.

Sometimes at night, I would lay awake and imagine leading my squad to a championship and earning a scholarship to a big-name school. I was excited at the opportunity to play point guard, but the pressure to do well was taking a toll on me.

Kevin walked into the weight room. I'd spotted him across the room as I did squats. My homie was a bit on the cocky side. He was 5'11', red-skinned, and tatted like a graffiti wall. "What it do, Jermaine?" he shouted.

Doug looked at me as he bit into a Snicker's. "I don't like that sissy," he said.

"'Ey, Doug, you might get some playing time this year," Kevin teased.

Doug gave him the finger. "Go bite one."

"I love you too, scrub!" he said.

At times, Kevin could be a pain in the ass. Every day at practice, we used to go at it hard. I knew it was going to be tough without him. Even though we fought at practice, it felt good having help at game time.

After doing squats, I worked on upper-body strengthening. While I was putting in work, Doug was across the room tripping out with his homies. I had worked up a mean sweat while doing arm curls. I was glistening under the lights in a wet T-shirt.

The veins popped out of my forearms and calves, making me hungrier. As I pushed myself to the limit, girls kept peeping through the door. They loved creeping around the weight room. There was something about being an athlete that lured the females. We called some of them "season whores" because depending on the season they'd make themselves available for action.

Kevin approached me. "What's popping?"

I dropped the 100-pound barbell to the floor and took a break. "I'm getting it in, bro-bro."

"Fo sheezy."

"You know you're wrong for quitting on us, right?"

"Basketball wasn't fulfilling to me. I was tired of going through the motions."

I wiped the sweat from my burning eyes. "I feel you on that one, Smitty. You have to follow your heart."

"Football is where my heart is," he said, patting his chest. "We got a game tonight, you know?"

"You starting?"

"Come on, J. You think I quit basketball to come off the bench?"

"Good luck, yo."

"Thanks," he said, heading out.

After he left, I skimmed the room for Doug. He was on the other side of the room chilling. I stood up and shouted, "Doug!"

"Yo?" he said, hopping off his lazy butt.

"Come spot me," I said.

Doug handed his boy a wad of cash and then ran over to spot me.

"What you got?" I said.

He smiled. "Some high potent weed. Let's go, I'm ready to go smoke this shit."

I shook my head. "How are you gonna be prepared for the season if you're always smoking out?"

"Easy, bruh."

I didn't understand the fetish of smoking trees and most of my homies did it like it was going out of style. "You go 'head," I said.

"Peace," he said, rushing out.

I laid on the weight bench staring at the ceiling. Sean McKenzie walked over and offered to spot me. He was the only white kid on the squad and he could ball. He could shoot the lights out. We nicknamed him White Chocolate because he had swagger. We worked out for a couple of hours and his mindset was on full focus like mine. I wasn't the only one looking forward to a breakout season.

Coach caught me on my way out the weight room. "Need a ride, kid?" he said.

"Thanks."

I hopped in Coach Baxter's Ford Expedition. His truck always smelled like Winter Fresh gum. I looked up to my coach. In a high school of predominately Blacks and Hispanics, he stood out in a good way. Coach was a great mentor and he reached out to us. He was someone that I trusted. I knew that he had good intentions for me. I could never forget the time he invited the team over to his house to have dinner with his family. It felt weird eating with them. Usually, the white people I came across were the ones in police uniforms that enjoyed roughing up innocent cats like me for no reason.

"Coach?" I said.

He looked at me as he tapped his fingers to a John Mayer song. "Speak your mind."

"I don't wanna play point guard. I'm comfortable playing at the two-spot."

"Why not? I think you can handle it. You're quick, you have great court vision, and you're an exceptional ball handler. I think it would be a great switch for you."

"Yeah but –"

"Believe in yourself; I believe in you. How's your foot?"

"Feels brand new. What are your expectations for the team this year?"

"The state title and nothing less."

"Huh?" I looked at him like he was crazy. I thought he was jiving but he was dead serious.

He turned his radio back up and focused his attention on the road. I thought he was insane.

We pulled into my driveway. I grabbed my book bag and basketball. "Thanks, Coach."

"No problem. Let me know if you need anything, kiddo."

"Okay."

"How are your grades coming along?"

"They could be better."

"Need a tutor?"

"Nah, I'm good," I said, hopping out of his truck.

My mother stepped outside as if she was expecting someone. Coach Baxter waved goodbye to her and then backed out the driveway.

Momma smiled and waved back. "Grab the mail," she said to me.

I checked the mailbox and handed her the mail. She seemed nervous as she searched through it.

"What are you looking for, Momma?"

"Here it is," she said, taking a deep breath.

I looked over her shoulder and read the letter with her: *Thank you for applying with the City of Miami Gardens but after further review . . .*

She ripped it in half before we could finish reading it.

Momma had been searching for a better paying job for over a year. Ever since she was laid off at Cigna Health Care, she had been juggling jobs. As of late, she had been pressing because the taxes on the house were due. "I don't know what to do . . . there are no jobs," she said, sounding upset. Then she walked in the house and closed the door.

I clutched the straps of my book bag and looked to the sky. Sometimes I wondered if there was a God, and if there was, I wondered why He made it so hard for us. All of a sudden, the ground began to tremble underneath my feet. It was Louie cruising by in his 550 Benz bumping Tupac's "Dear Mama." The bling around Louie's neck and wrist was gleaming like his rims. I turned my cap a few inches to the side while he studied me. He had it all. His life seemed like a fairy tale that every cat on the block envied. There were times I wished I had it good like him too. I would've given my life in order for Momma not to struggle.

After he left the block, I went in the house to check on Momma. She was in her bedroom looking at TV.

I took off my cap and sat on the bed. "Momma, I'm gonna look for a job this weekend."

She looked at me. "No, I want you to concentrate on school; you have all your life to work. Education is the only way you're going to make it in this world. I didn't have anyone to encourage me to go to school; I wish I had though."

"I'm smart enough to do both. I wanna help."

She shook her head. "If you start slipping, that's it."

I grinned. "I'm too fresh to get caught slipping."

"Uh huh."

WSVN 7-News broadcasted the stabbing at my school. I watched the ill expression on Momma's face. She shook her head. "I can't imagine what that poor child's mother is going through right now."

The news showed footage of Pablo's mother pleading for someone to come forward.

"All this violence in the schools doesn't make sense. I tell you one thing, kids aren't the same as they used to be. This generation of children is something else," Momma said disgustedly.

Here we go, I thought.

"I better not catch your name in no mess out to that school."

"Trust me, you won't, Momma," I said, feeling guilty.

2

I FOUND ME A PART-TIME GIG at a detail shop. I wasn't too proud to work. Every day it was extremely hot but I adjusted to the heat. I'd keep a bottle of water on hand and work my butt off till the sun went down. The girls made my job easy. They'd come to work in their itty-bitty shorts, commanding attention. They got it too. Dudes coming through the wash were captured at the sight of skin. I went to school with one of the hotties; Nia was gorgeous. She had a cute chocolate face, a big booty, and bone-straight hair. I never had the nerve to step to her because she was high maintenance.

One day, I went inside the office to refill my bottle with cold water. My body was drenched with sweat. Jay-Z and Alicia Keys was on the radio singing "In New York." I grabbed a chair and gulped down some water. Then I relaxed for a couple of minutes while I sang the song on the radio.

Nia and Beverley looked at me. "No no, boo, you're supposed to be working," Beverley said.

I turned my cap to the back and looked at her like she couldn't be serious. "Mind your business; I don't see you over there doing no work either, Miss Thing." I ignored them and closed my eyes.

Nia came and sat on my lap. "Why do you always wear a stupid hat? You must have something to hide." She took off my cap and laughed at my nappy hair.

I reached for my cap. "No, it's a habit."

"A habit to hide the fact that you can't afford a haircut?"

"I'll get one every week if you give me a kiss."

She looked down at my raggedy shoes. "In your dreams," she said, throwing the cap in my face. Then she got up and started shaking her thing to "Rude Boy" by Rihanna.

I fantasized her and I getting it on. "One day you're gonna want a brother like me," I sighed, as she teased me with her hips.

"Boy, please, you'll never get a taste of this chocolate pudding. Cute and broke is played out, boo-boo." She and Beverly gave each other high five.

Tim came out of his office and everybody scrambled. "What in heaven's name is going on?" he said.

I ran back outside before he started threatening to fire everybody again.

As I vacuumed out a line of cars, Louie pulled into the car wash. His Benz caught all the attention. He let down his window and looked at me. "Hey, amigo, lemme get the Platinum wash. Is that hokay?" His English was horrible.

"No sweat, bro."

He stepped out of the car, looking suave.

I vacuumed out his ride and then rolled it to the back to be detailed. It was the first time I'd ever driven a Benz. It was all that and more. I felt like I was in a spaceship with all the controls on board. I started bobbing my head to his Akon CD. Then I looked in the mirror and started singing the words to "Smack That."

All of a sudden, the music stopped. Tim had opened the passenger's side door and turned off the radio. "One more warning! I'm telling you, I'm gon' clear everybody outta this place!" he said.

I hopped out of the car and got back to work. After we were finished detailing the car, I went back inside to turn in Louie's keys. He was standing at the cash register talking to Nia. For the first time in my life, I felt like a loser.

Nia walked outside with Louie. She had a big smile on her face as she leaned over in his ride. When she came back inside the office, she started bragging to her girls.

"The dope dealers always get the fly chicks," Otis said, shaking his head.

"Man, forget these girls; they ain't about nothing." I headed out the door and got back to work.

* * *

I had quit my job because Tim shortchanged me. He wouldn't pay me for half the hours I had worked. My first paycheck was $36.85 after taxes. I wanted to swing on that cat because I had planned on helping Momma with the bills around the house.

There was an old man at the park watching me take out my frustrations on the goal. I threw the ball off the backboard and went for a two-handed dunk. It ricocheted off the rim and bounced over to the bench where the old man was sitting. He reached down for my ball.

"I got it," I said, inhaling his odor. "Ew, man, you need a bath."

He started coughing. Then he spat out a yellow ball of mucus.

"Man, come on, that's nasty." I shook my head and walked away.

"What's ya name?" he said.

I smirked. "Why you ask?"

He pointed at the ball. "You remind me of myself when I was a young boy."

I looked at him like he was crazy. "Psyche!"

"I used to be good back in the day. I was unstoppable," he said, smiling. His teeth were stained brown.

"I think you may wanna keep your mouth closed."

He kept rambling on. "I haven't touched a basketball in over thirty years . . . ." All of a sudden, his eyes became glassy.

I tossed him the ball out of pity but he let it drop to the ground. "Fine with me, bro," I said and ran back on the court. I started hitting jumpers all over the place. I was in a rhythm.

The old man stood up and started clapping. "Bravo!"

He made me shoot a brick. After I chased down the rebound, he stepped on the court. The old man acted like he wanted to challenge me to a game. "You don't want none of this ass whooping," I said, weaving the rock between my legs.

"Give me a shot, young blood," he said. He took off his dirty coat and held out his hands for the ball. His arms were scarred with needle marks.

I tossed him the ball and he shot it. The old man had good form on his shot but he missed badly. I got the rebound. Before I could give it back to him for another shot, he'd put back on his coat. "Don't you want another shot?" I said.

"Sometimes you only get one shot," he mumbled as he walked away.

* * *

For some reason the old man's words had stuck with me for weeks. Basketball season was creeping up fast. I felt it was my "one shot" to get into a good college and make Momma proud of me. I wanted to major in Business or whatever field made a lot of bread. Sometimes I dreamed of making it to the NBA, but I didn't wanna get caught up in hoop dreams. There were too many brothers sitting at home anticipating a call from the NBA. I'd seen it happen too many times. Every day those same dudes hung around school flossing, like they were still on top of the world. It was pitiful to watch because some of them chumps had knees that were through dealing. Most of them didn't wanna come to grips with reality. I refused to be the same.

After school, I had hit the gym. I was on fire. No one could guard me one-on-one. We were playing five-on-five street ball. Everybody was dancing with the ball, trying to display their best moves. Chris dribbled the ball back and forth behind his back, talking crap to me.

Last year, he took my spot in the starting lineup after I got hurt. Ever since then, he thought he was the baddest cat on the court.

I stole the ball from him and passed it to Doug. Doug started showboating with the ball too, as we scrambled to get open. My homie found me for the alley-oop. Everyone under the basket cleared the lane except for Six-Nine. He got served a facial.

Six-Nine pushed me as I dangled on the rim. "Man, get your nuts out my face!" he said, upset.

I hopped down, feeling good. "That boy got ups!" I said, teasing him.

"You pushed off!"

I banged on my chest while backpedaling full speed down court. "Man up, chump!"

"Next time I'ma pack yo' shit out the gym!"

I laughed in his face. "Y'all can't stop me!" I shouted.

Everybody was talking junk.

More people had filed into the gym to watch us hoop. Open gym had become live entertainment for a bunch of spectators. Coach Baxter was seated high in the stands scouting his talent for this year. A Miami-Dade College recruiter was chilling in the stands too. I was getting a feel for our revamped squad. Two of last year's starters had graduated and taken their game to FAMU and Bethune Cookman College. It felt strange without Kevin in the gym, but I'd accepted the fact that he was gone. Finally, I was ready to accept my role as starting point guard. My dream of leading the team to its first state title was at hand.

I felt like the chosen one.

Everyone in the gym had their eyes on me. The oohs and aahs had given me a rush of adrenalin as I made it rain. "Game!" I shouted after hitting a fade-away jumper.

"One more game," my homies begged me.

"Y'all cats can't see me," I said, shaking my head.

"He ain't nothin' but a pussy," Six-Nine said.

"You still talking trash? Aren't you tired of nuts in your face?"

Everybody started cracking up.

"He got you on that one, homie," White Chocolate said.

I grabbed my bag and headed out the gym. Someone shouted my name from the opposite end of the hall.

"You staying for the game tonight?" Kevin said.

"You know it."

I hit the shower and changed clothes. Then I watched the J.V. game with my homies: Bones, Doug, and Floyd. Bones and Floyd were two thugs that had dropped out of school. They made a living hustling on the block and burglarizing homes. Bones had long locks, while Floyd kept a low haircut.

They were two savages.

All of us stood below the stands and watched the cute girls file in for the varsity game. Doug tried to kick game to all the girls while we watched him get dissed. Most of the girls were into dudes with paper.

Nia walked past me with her girls like she didn't see me. *It's all good*, I thought.

The stadium was packed at the start of varsity's game. Everyone was hyped as the band got down. At kickoff, Kevin received the ball. He juked past the first three defenders and found an open seam up the middle. My homie was in a foot race with one defender on his heels. Everyone in the stands stood up as the pursuit was on. Kevin stiff-handed the boy and broke free for the end zone.

The stadium exploded.

"That's my dawg!" I shouted.

Kevin folded his arms and posed as if he was the business.

"Goddamn! That man is a beast," Bones said, shaking his head.

"I bet you my homie returns another one before the night's over," I said, hyped up.

"Yeah, ain't no stopping that joker with that kinda speed. Buddy reminds me of Devin Hester," Floyd added, giving him props.

"Man, y'all mofos trippin', that was only one play," Doug said, unimpressed.

Floyd pulled out a stack. "Then put your money where your mouth is, partner."

I laughed when Doug got quiet. "Don't get quiet now," I said.

All game long, Kevin made play after play. Hands down, he was the best receiver on the field. One play, he got smacked across the middle. The *clack* could be heard from the stands. Everyone in the stands shouted, "Oooh!"

"See that's why I'ont play football. I get hit like that, I'm gettin' back up swingin', dawg."

Kevin hopped up and started jawing with the free safety.

I laughed. "That's my dawg!"

A couple of seconds later, I saw Ashley walking up the steps. She had smooth caramel-colored skin and a nicely toned body. The girl was smart too. Every day, Ashley rocked pretty dresses and heels. She was the perfect definition of a girly-girl.

"What's up, girl?" Doug said.

"Ugh are you talking to me?"

"Yes."

"Please don't," she said and kept walking.

"Dayum," we all said.

After the game, I called Kevin over. "Good game, homie," I said.

Everyone else gave him love, too, except for Doug.

"Appreciate it, y'all." Kevin looked at me. "Hey, don't leave. I got this party I want you to come check out with me tonight," he said, running to catch up with his team.

"Alright."

* * *

My alarm clock sounded at 6:45 a.m. I went to the bathroom and brushed my teeth. Then I started to get ready for school until I realized it was Sunday. After I came to my senses, I laid back down. Last night's party had me wasted. I got a few digits and got into a big fight too. A cat at the party got mad because his girl was on my jock. It was too much drama for one night. I knew it was best for me to fall back. Hanging out and partying was a wrap.

I got out of bed at one o' clock. I fixed me a bowl of cereal, grabbed the Sports section out of the morning paper, and headed back to my room. The back page had a list of Miami Dade County's top basketball prospects. I'd made the list and it felt good.

I sat on the bed, munching on my Frosted Flakes while I read the caption under my name: *Jermaine Parker is expected back after sustaining a right foot injury. He will be expected to carry the load for the Bulls after the departure of standout point guard Kevin Smith . . . .*

The paper had me listed at 6'4", 190 pounds. They'd given me a few extra pounds but I was cool with it. As I read the paper, someone banged on my door. I tossed the paper to the side and got the door.

Roy looked upset. "You took my newspaper?" he said.

"No, it's on the table."

"I'm missing a section," he said, biting down on his bottom lip. "You wouldn't happen to know where it is, would you?"

"Oh my bad, yo. You need to chill, it's not the end of the world." I grabbed the paper off my bed and handed it to him. "You happy?"

Roy snapped and kicked the door. "You ain't gonna be livin' in my house and disrespecting me all the time."

My tone went up a notch. "Then I will get out your house, man! You ain't saying shit."

"You ain't nothing but a li'l mama's boy walking around here like you the man. You ain't shit but another nigga with a field of dreams. You need to get a job and stop dreaming, motherfucker."

"Man, kiss my ass!"

He grabbed my throat with two hands and threw me up against the wall. I pushed his big pudgy body off me. Roy had me beat by a hundred pounds. Even though he was short, he was strong. We fought it out like two grown men going for the kill.

Momma came running out of her room when she heard things falling and breaking. "Get off my baby!" she yelled. My two sisters rushed out of their rooms and watched in fear.

Roy brushed me across the wall. "I'm tired of you fucking with me!" he said.

All of my mother's pictures that hung in the hallway were scattered across the floor. My mother started throwing licks at Roy. He shoved her out the way and threw more punches at me. He connected twice as I swung back. I felt my teeth sink deep into my bottom lip. Blood spilled out of the cut like a running faucet.

"Y'all please stop it!" Momma screamed. Somehow, she found the strength and broke us apart before Roy killed me.

I stormed out of the house. Bloodied face, I ran across the street to see if Doug was home. I needed his gun because I was gonna blow my stepfather's brains out. When no one answered, I ran three blocks to see if he was to his girlfriend's house. It wasn't over until I saw Roy suffer in pain. As I ran the streets barefoot and shirtless, I was stopped by a police officer. Luckily, it was a cool one who I knew.

Officer Cruz looked me up and down. "Everything's okay?"

"Yeah."

He didn't seem convinced as blood trickled down my chest. "Get in the car. I'm taking you home."

"No, I can't go home. I might kill somebody," I said, breathing hard.

"Whoa, hold on now, calm down. What's going on? Talk to me."

I started pacing because he was holding me up.

Officer Cruz got out of the car and spoke calmly. "Just talk to me. Come on, Jermaine, you know I'm on your side." He already knew my situation. He'd been called out to our crib on other occasions due to domestic disputes involving Roy and I.

"My stepdaddy jumped on me and I'ma kill his ass!"

"You have a lot going for yourself. I would hate to see you throw it all away on a piece of shit. Think about it: do you want to spend the rest of your life in jail?"

"No . . ."

He patted me on the back. "Smart kid."

Officer Cruz made me get in the back seat of his car, and then handed me a towel to clean myself up. I looked in the mirror at my face. My eye was swollen and my bottom lip was fat.

Officer Cruz handed me his cell phone. "Why don't you call a friend or relative to see if you can stay with them until things cool off? Or you could make a report and have Mr. Tough Guy take a ride with me."

"No, it's his house; I just need to go get a few things."

When we pulled up to the house, Roy was sitting outside drinking a forty-ounce like nothing happened. Officer Cruz followed me into the house.

"Real motherfuckers don't talk to the police," Roy said.

"I suggest you keep quiet," Officer Cruz said.

Roy trailed us inside of the house. My mother was sitting in the front room. She hopped up, seeming relieved. Then she hugged me. "Are you okay, baby?"

"I'm good."

"Stop babying him all the time, Janice," Roy said.

"Roy, please!" she said.

"Both of y'all can hit the road, damn it!"

I walked in my room and started throwing clothes into a garbage bag. Momma stood in my room begging me not to leave.

"Let him go!" Roy shouted from the hallway.

Momma grabbed my arm tightly. "Just let me talk to him, Jermaine."

I threw on a white tee and some jeans. "No, I gotta go. Talking to him ain't gonna do any good. He's gonna always nitpick because he's not my father."

"Please don't go. Do it for me."

"No disrespect, Momma, but I'll be doggone if I stay here and put up with that fool."

"Don't tell me no. You must've forgotten I'm your mama and you're my responsibility."

I held the bag across my shoulder. "I can take care of myself."

"Jermaine, be serious. It's hard out there, baby. Officer, please tell him."

Officer Cruz looked away as if he didn't wanna get involved.

"I can make it on my own." I kissed Momma on the cheek. "Sorry, I have to go."

"What are you going to do? Sell drugs on the street corner with your friends?" She started crying as I walked out of my bedroom with my things.

My mind was set. I walked out of the house without turning back.

3

———

My coach reached out to me and offered me a place to stay. One simple phone call was all it had taken. Officer Cruz drove me across town to Coach Baxter's house. The area he lived in was a long stretch from the hood: nice homes, palm trees, and green grass were natural scenery. The sight of bar less homes and banks was like a breath of fresh air.

I felt like Coach's house was the best option for now. I could've stayed with my grandmother but she had too much hell going on in her house too. My two cousins lived with her and one of them had a bunch of kids. It would've been too much of a struggle to live with Grandma and stay focused on school.

I felt like a bum knocking at my coach's door. I waved bye to Officer Cruz when Coach Baxter opened the door. He let me in and showed me where to put my things. The room that he had for me was nice. It had a big bathroom in it too.

"Go ahead and get freshened up."

"Okay."

"Shout if you need anything," he said, closing the door.

I grabbed a clean set of towels off the bed and took a shower. After I put on clothes, I peeped out the blinds. Coach Baxter's wife and 10-year-old son were getting out of a Volkswagen station wagon. Coach walked outside and hugged his wife and son.

He and his wife spent several minutes outside talking. I assumed that I was the topic of their conversation.

After fifteen minutes, a red Mustang pulled up at the curb. A tanned brunette got out on the passenger's side. She appeared like a spoiled rotten white girl. She had long straight hair and a perfect thin hourglass-shaped body. I already knew I didn't wanna cross her path. I backed away from the window when I saw them coming.

"What's for dinner tonight?" the little boy yelled.

I stretched out on the bed and started twirling my basketball on a finger. The sun was beginning to go down while I spent time thinking of home. I was ready to go back to the hood. Coach Baxter's neighborhood was too peaceful and quiet for me; the only action was dogs barking and birds chirping.

At seven o'clock, Coach stuck his head in the door. "Dinner's ready," he said.

"Is everything okay?"

"Of course. We're happy to have you."

I got up and followed him to the dining room. His wife was setting the table. Mrs. Baxter smiled at me and said, "I hope you like what we're having for dinner."

I pulled out a chair. "Mrs. Baxter, I'm so hungry that I could eat an elephant."

Coach laughed. "Well, have a seat," he said, patting my shoulder. He called upstairs for the rest of his family.

The little boy rushed down and sat at the table. He stared at me like I was an alien.

Coach re-introduced me to his son, Ethan. "You remember Jermaine from the time we ate dinner with the team, right?" he said.

"I think so."

"What's up, Ethan?" I said.

He waved shyly.

"Lindsey, honey, we're waiting on you!" Coach Baxter shouted.

A minute later, his daughter pranced downstairs with an iPhone glued to her ear. She walked into the dining room and stopped as if she had seen a ghost.

I was cracking up inside because I could read her thoughts: *Where did this black guy come from?*

Coach introduced me to her.

"Nice to meet you," I said.

She half-smiled and looked at her peeps as if she was confused. "Why is he here?" she blurted out.

"Honey, sit down and eat," Mrs. Baxter said.

"Sure, whatever. It would be nice to know what's going on around here sometimes."

"Lindsey, stop being rude," her mother said.

"Can someone pass me the rolls?" Lindsey said.

I handed her the rolls.

She gave me a fake smile and said, "Thank you."

Coach looked at me. "The constant usage of cell phones may cause the brain to malfunction at times, get my drift?"

"Dad, don't start, okay?" Lindsey said.

"You see." He winked at me

I shrugged my shoulders, avoiding the drama.

Dinner was so-so. I had to force down my food because it was flavorless. The meatloaf didn't have gravy and the carrots were yucky. The dinner rolls filled my gut though.

"Mom, can we have chicken tomorrow?" Ethan said.

Everybody paused for some strange reason.

"Sure why not?" Mrs. Baxter said, clearing her throat.

"May I suggest Popeyes? I haven't had their chicken in a long time," I said.

A smile spread across everybody's face.

Coach got up from the table. "Let's go watch film," he said.

I was about to take my plate in the kitchen but he made me leave it. I felt as though I had broken a cardinal rule because at my crib everybody had to clean up after themselves. I followed

Coach into the living room. He had a big-screen HD TV. We watched film for about an hour. He pointed out a few things that I needed to work on like my defense. I openly accepted the criticism because I already knew that I could get lazy on defense.

"Scoring comes easy for you but once you perfect your game on both ends, you're going to be unstoppable like Lebron James ... I see a lot of potential in you." He rewound the tape to where I'd let my man beat me off the dribble, scoring a lay-up inside of the paint. "See, that's what we have to limit this year." He hopped up and led me outside. Then he grabbed a basketball out of his truck. "Look here," he said. He bent his legs and started sliding across the driveway.

I wasn't up for it tonight. "Coach, are you serious? It's late and it's mosquitoes out here." I killed one before it landed on my arm.

"I'm very serious, now come on."

"I'm serious, too, it's mad mosquitoes out here," I said, killing another one.

"Once you get moving they'll buzz off."

I laughed because I couldn't believe Coach was outside in his pajamas tripping.

"You're going to be a great player; you just don't know it yet," he said.

I bent my knees and started sliding across the driveway with Coach. We stayed outside for two hours. Finally, Mrs. Baxter came outside and put an end to Coach's madness.

* * *

All week, it was the same thing. Coach was working me to death and the season hadn't even started. He made me embrace defense and that was exactly what I had begun to do.

One evening, I sat on my bed, looking over the answers to the math test I'd failed. My average was an F after getting a 40 percent. I knew my GPA was gonna take a huge dip. I talked to my teacher and he advised me to get a tutor. I knew Momma would've flipped if she knew I was slipping again. I put aside the test because everything looked foreign. My mother was on my mind and I couldn't concentrate like I needed to. I hadn't talked to her over the phone in days, and we hadn't seen each other since I'd left home. I missed her to death but I refused to go back home. I hated Roy. Every time I looked in the mirror and saw the scar above my lip, I hated him more.

I felt bad because I couldn't help my mother. I knew she didn't wanna be with Roy, but she didn't have no other place to go. It was tearing me apart inside.

I put on my headphones and started listening to Drizzy. His lyrics had me bouncing off the wall. I felt like I had to do something to make it happen. Everything crossed my mind; I thought of selling everything from crack to marijuana. Then I thought about serving time in jail. That was one place I never wanted to go, so I cancelled out the thought of standing on a street corner.

Just then, Ethan walked in the room. He smiled at me.

"What's up, Ethan?" I said, removing my headphones.

"What are you listening to?"

"You ever heard of Drake?"

"Yeah, he's awesome. Can I listen?"

I put the headphones on his ears. "There you go, li'l bro."

Lindsey peeped in the room. "Ethan, you little dweeb, what are you doing?" She looked at me as if she was sorry. "He can be a real pest sometimes."

"He's alright." I started spinning the ball on the tip of my finger.

Ethan's eyes stretched wide open. "Cool!"

A blond-haired girl walked in the room and introduced herself to me.

"Nice to meet you, Heidi," I said.

"So, like, where are you from?" she said.

"Liberty City."

"How is it?"

"How is what?"

"The hood?"

Lindsey rolled her eyes. "Heidi, please stop asking stupid questions."

"Well, anyway, we're going swimming, would you like to come?"

I shrugged. "Sure."

I followed them to the backyard. Lindsey and her friends took advantage of her parents while they weren't home. The music was turned up loud and there were a couple of white boys dangling their feet in the deep end of the water. A third girl entered the pool area from the patio. She had a bottle of beer in her hand. She tossed it to one of the boys and then dove into the pool. I felt out of place because hanging with white folks was new to me. One thing I noticed was they knew how to have a good time without all the drama.

Two more girls came in the backyard and enjoyed the fun. A blue-eyed, freckled-face boy got out of the pool and threw one of the girls in the water with all her clothes on.

"Austin, you fucking idiot! I'm going to kill you!" she screamed.

Austin stood by me and said, "Dude, you're not getting in?"

"I guess so." I sat down at the table and took off my shoes.

Lindsey took off her T-shirt.

"Dude, she's hot," Austin said, watching her every move.

Lindsey had on a black bikini, which made her evenly tanned skin glow. She stuck her pink-polished toes into the water to check its temperature. "Oh my gosh, you guys, the water is so frigging cold . . ."

Austin reached over me and turned up the radio. "This song rocks!" he said. A caller had requested "Good Life" by a group called One Republic.

Lindsey walked over to the table and started putting on sun block. She looked at me when I took off my shirt. "You may want to put this on," she said, squeezing the lotion in my hands.

"Thank you." I rubbed it on even though I didn't think I needed it. Then I jumped in the pool like everyone else. Lindsey was the only one acting too cute to get in. She laid on a pool chair and soaked up the sun, while we swam and had fun.

An hour later, a curly-haired blond boy came in the backyard. He and Lindsey started arguing. They left the pool area and took it to the front. I didn't pay them any mind while I floated on top of the water.

"Brad really needs to get a fucking life and leave her alone," one of the girls said.

"What do you care?" the beer-drinking boy said. He wrapped his arms around the girl's neck and started tonguing her down.

I got out of the pool and sat on the edge while they got freaky. Ethan stuck his head out the sliding glass door and peeped the action. They saw him staring and threw a flip-flop towards the window. "Beat it, you little prick," the girl said.

Ethan scrammed.

After I was dry, I went back in the house. I saw a red Mustang peel out through the front room window. Lindsey walked in the house and slammed the door, crying.

"What's wrong?" I said.

"Nothing, just leave me alone."

"My bad," I said, walking into the guest room. I took a hot shower and then chilled.

*   *   *

That night, Coach didn't get home until late. He tapped on the door at ten o' clock, awaking me from a good dream about Ms. Love. "Sorry if I woke you," he said, shutting the door and leaving.

At three in the morning, I heard my door open again. "Hey," a soft voice whispered.

"Yes?" I said.

Lindsey closed the door and had the nerve to sit on the bed. "Sorry for waking you."

I sat up and moved away. "Whoa, hold up now," I said.

"Will you relax? I just came in here to apologize for earlier. Sometimes I can be a real bitch."

"Don't sweat it. I understand you were upset."

"Why are guys such jerks?"

"Hmmm, that's a good question. I guess it's because some-times we don't realize when we have a good thing."

"Well, it's too late for him to apologize. He sleeps with my best friend and expects to come crawling back . . ."

"That's not cool at all, yo."

She began crying.

"On the flipside you're a perfect ten and you don't have to settle for less," I said.

She laughed and wiped the tears away. "Oh my gosh, it's like you know the right things to say."

"I keep it real, shorty."

She reached out her arms. "Can I please give you a hug?"

"Yeah," I said, feeling uncomfortable.

She gave me a friendly hug and then got up. "Thank you so much."

"You're welcome."

She waved goodbye and walked out of the room. After she left out, I laid down and drifted back to sleep.

* * *

A week later, I started my conditioning. Doug and I ran the track. It was scorching hot. My homie made it halfway around the track then gave out.

"Come on, Doug," I said, jogging in place.

He stretched out on the grass. "Go 'head. It's too goddamn hot."

"You're out of shape, bro."

"I'm coming. Give me a few minutes."

"Stop being lazy."

"One more minute."

"Man, forget you." My stamina allowed me to go three more laps. Doug had hauled tail on me. After I finished, I headed inside of the gym. I relaxed and watched everybody shoot around while I waited on Coach.

"Let's get a quick game," Doug said, motioning me to the floor.

I gulped down a cold bottle of water. "Nah, I'm tired."

"Come on, dawg."

I shook my head. "Not today."

They got the drift and started playing without me. White Chocolate was balling. He threw a perfect lob over the top and Chris threw it down, two hands, over Doug.

I hopped up because it was sweet. "Ooh woo!" I said. I wasn't the only one who thought Chris' dunk was off the charts.

Candace, the girl's star point guard, had hopped up too. "That was sick! The boy got hops," she said, looking at me.

"For real."

Coach walked in the gym. He looked at me and said, "Let's go."

I grabbed my things and headed out of the gym. "Is everything good, Coach?"

He sighed. "We need to get you a math tutor fast or we're going to have a big problem. I know you have a lot going on outside of school, but you're going to have to find a way to block it out."

I shook my head in frustration because I knew that I was slipping. Too much stress had me tripping.

"Hang in there, kid. We're going to get you help. You hear me?"

"Yeah."

Coach gripped the back of my neck. "Good."

* * *

After that day, I had to spend 45 minutes with a math tutor five days a week after school. I wasn't allowed to work out or participate in open gym until I brought up my GPA to a 2.0. I was mad at the world. But looking on the bright side, my tutor was fine. She was the same age as me, but way ahead of the learning curve. "Jermaine, you have to concentrate," Ashley said.

I looked at her pretty face. "Anyone ever told you that you favor Meagan Goode?"

She slammed her pencil down as if she was aggravated. "Jermaine! You have to try and get this. Now come on, it's not hard."

"I'm sorry. It's hard to concentrate with you sitting across from me."

"I know I'm beautiful but get over it."

I paid attention as she broke down the steps of simplifying radical expressions. The way she explained everything made sense. But whether or not I could work the problems on a test remained to be seen.

After my evening's tutoring session, I walked Ashley to her car. She had a brand-new Honda Accord; the paper tag was still on it.

I set her books on the back seat. Then I leaned inside of her window as she cranked up the car. "Thank you," I said.

"You're welcome. I hope you do well tomorrow."

"I hope so too." I looked into her eyes, overcoming the butterflies in my stomach. "Can I take you out this weekend?"

"Yes. What time will you be picking me up?" she said, fixing her bangs in the mirror.

"Uh, I guess at eight."

"Sounds good."

"Alright, cutie."

Ashley put the car in reverse. I moved out of the way and watched her leave. For the first time in a while, she had me excited about going out on a date. After all, I needed to get out and have some fun.

* * *

Friday night, I called Ashley from Doug's crib. Her tone changed when I asked her to pick me up because I didn't have a car. "I'm coming," she said.

I waited for three hours.

When ten o' clock rolled around, I figured she wasn't coming. I called her cell phone and she wouldn't pick up. "I can't believe this girl," I said.

Doug thought it was funny. "No money, no honey," he said. "You know these hoes not checkin' for you if you ain't got no ride."

I brushed off his jokes while I watched TV.

Later that night, I called my mother when I saw her pull in the driveway. "Hey, Momma, what's up?" I said.

"Where are you, Jermaine?"

"I'm across the street at Doug's house."

"Oh Lord. Of all people in the world."

"We aren't doing anything."

"Why won't you come back home? I miss you."

"So Roy can keep kicking me out? I love you to pieces, Momma, but I'm not coming back."

"Jermaine, you can't bounce from house to house like you don't have a home. You need to be settled in one place, so you can concentrate on school."

I got quiet.

"Can you at least go stay with Nana so I'll know you're okay?"

"Yes, ma'am, if that will make you happy." I knew I couldn't live with Coach Baxter for too long. I took into consideration that he had a family of his own.

* * *

Monday morning, I got my math test back. When I flipped it over and saw an 80 percent, I almost died. Too bad it wasn't my test. My teacher had handed me someone else's test and snatched it back.

"That's messed up, man," I said.

He walked to the other side of the room handing out tests. I was nervous as he headed back towards me. He leaned my way but reached over me.

I shook my head. "Come on, Mr. Thomas. Why you playing?"

Finally, he handed me back my test. "Good job. Keep it up," he said.

My mouth dropped open when I saw a 90 percent. "Oh, I am. You can believe that, Mr. Thomas."

After class, I saw Ashley in the hallway. I gave her a bear hug, overlooking the fact that she had played me. Getting an A on my math test was perfectly good enough for me. "Thank you, shorty," I said.

She pushed me away and fixed her hair. "Please don't ever do that again."

"My bad, shorty."

"No problem," she said and walked away.

My day was going good until I saw Doug being walked down the hall in handcuffs. He had a stone cold look on his face. Everybody standing in the hallway was told to clear out. Two police officers escorted him out of the building. I followed them outside and watched at the door. My principal threatened to suspend everyone who wasn't in class. I couldn't care less as I watched my homie get thrown into the back seat of a police car. At that moment, word got around school that Doug was looking at serious jail time. His wrongdoing had come back to haunt him. I was told that Pablo had identified him right before he died. I was hurt because it was two lost lives. My heart was heavy and my eyes were holding back tears. Doug was like a brother to me. It was hard not to feel the pain. I said a prayer for my homie and hoped my name stayed clear in the process.

4.

———

EVERY NIGHT I TOSSED AND turned in my sleep. My homie was looking at life and I prayed that I didn't get caught up in the mix. There wasn't a second, I didn't wish that Pablo were alive, and Doug was free. That wasn't the only thing on my mind. The fact that I didn't have a place to call home bothered me too. I refused to call my grandmother because I knew the conditions at her house weren't favorable for me. At the same time I couldn't take living with my coach any longer. I felt like a caged bird. I appreciated Coach taking me in but I missed being around my peoples. There was no place like home. Three weeks away from the block seemed like an eternity, but through all the stress and pain, basketball kept me sane. I stayed focused on getting better.

One late night, the rain started to pour down as I hit jumpers at the park. Lightning lit up the black sky and the sound of thunder rumbled through the air. The raindrops refused to yield; they beat down on me till I was soaked. Puddles of rain had drenched my shoes but I kept stroking jumpers.

A car pulled up at the park while I lit it up. Someone got out of the car in a raincoat. As they got closer, I recognized that it was Coach Baxter. I couldn't believe he'd found me. At twelve o'clock in the morning, I expected him to be at home with his family. I figured he was worried because I wasn't in school yesterday. I had spent that day getting high with Bones and Floyd. It was my first time falling to the temptation of smoking weed. At that moment, it helped me cope with my problems.

Coach threw a jacket over my shoulders. "Oh, thank heavens you're all right. We were worried sick about you. Come on," he said, walking me to the car.

I found it hard to believe that he cared so much.

Coach took me to get a bite to eat and then took me to his home. When we pulled in the driveway, he looked at me. "If you ever need to talk, I'm here for you. Understand me?"

I nodded as I looked out the window

"Keep your head up, kid," he said, stepping out of the car.

I tried my best to take his advice, as I got out of the car, and headed into the house.

* * *

A couple of days later, I went to the jail with Doug's mother. I had to see him. It was the only way I could sleep at night. When he walked out, it was hard to read him. He looked at me as if he knew he had screwed up. We stared at each other through a glass window for a few seconds. Then we both reached for the telephone. "What's going on?" he said.

"I miss you, bro."

"Don't be gettin' all soft on me, dawg."

I looked down because I didn't want him to see the tears in my eyes.

"Hold your head up. I did wrong and I gotta pay for it."

I looked at him and placed a hand on the glass. "I love you, bro."

He set his hand on the same spot. "I luh you too and I wanna read your name in the paper."

I smiled. "You better believe it."

5

I spent the weekend studying in my room. I had a math test coming up and I couldn't afford to fall behind. Playing catch-up wasn't my thing especially in math. As I sat on the floor working out problems, I couldn't get the hang of it. It was too complicated. I tried to refer to my notes but that wasn't working either. Frustration began to kick in. I threw my books against the wall.

Lindsey stuck her head in my bedroom. "Holy shit what was that? Are you okay?" she said.

I gathered my book and my papers out of the corner. "I'm cool."

She didn't seem convinced. "Do you need any help?"

"Are you good in math?"

Lindsey walked in the room. "Depends. What kind of math is it?"

"Algebra II."

She sat on the floor Indian-style and began reading over the problems in my book.

"Okay, I remember this . . ." She worked out a few problems and they matched the answers in the back of the book.

"I still don't get it," I sighed.

She slowed down and showed me step-by-step while her phone rang every five minutes.

After an hour, I had it down pat. I closed my book, feeling relieved. "Thank you very much for your help. I owe you big time."

"Relax, it's no big deal." She smiled. "What do you like to do for fun?"

"Play basketball."

"That's it?"

"Yep, that's it."

"That's no fun. Do you have a girlfriend?"

"Nah."

"Why not? I mean you seem like a pretty cool guy to me."

I shrugged. "Thanks."

She got up and swung her long bouncy hair from side to side. "Are you going to stay locked up in this room or go out and have some fun tonight?"

"I'm cool. I don't hang out."

"No way. You're coming out with me and I'm not taking no for an answer."

"Well, I guess I don't have a choice."

I ended up going to a party with Lindsey and her two friends. It was crazy. Everyone had taken the word fun to another level. Lady Gaga was on blast and the majority of the crowd was getting their drink on. There were a few weed heads in the spot too. One boy was so high that he jumped off the two-story roof and belly flopped into the pool.

For two straight hours, I chilled and watched everyone get wasted. Even though I enjoyed the party, it felt weird being the only black person. Other than that complaint, I thought it was cool that I didn't have to watch my back. There was no fighting and everybody was cool. One red-haired boy tossed me a beer. "Drink up, my dude!" he said.

After I took a few sips, I went into the kitchen and threw it in the garbage. Beer was not my thing. I poured a shot of tequila and washed it down, as I peeped out the action in the kitchen. A bunch of crazy white boys had a beer-drinking contest. One boy drank a liter of beer in 7.2 seconds.

"Whoa," I said, shocked.

One of the boys turned to me. "He's a fucking gun!"

Lindsey walked into the kitchen with a different friend. Her friend stared at me as if she wanted me. It tickled me when she whispered in Lindsey's ear. A few seconds later, the blond short-haired girl approached me. "Hi," she said.

"Hello."

"I'm Jennifer." She seemed like an airhead.

Lindsey pulled her away. "What are you doing?" she said.

The girl resisted. "I'm talking right now, do you mind?"

"Fine, have it your way, Jenny." Lindsey stormed out of the kitchen.

Jennifer looked at me confused. "What was that all about?"

"Beats me, yo."

After a few minutes, Jennifer grabbed my hand. "Let's dance," she said, pulling me into the living room when "OMG" by Usher came on. She was all over me. The girl was a handful.

I put my hands on Jennifer's hips while she rubbed her bottom against me. She gave me a boner. "Oh my," she grinned slyly.

Lindsey grabbed me and said, "Let's go!"

"Right now?" I said.

"Yes, right now."

I got in the car and Lindsey sped off. She seemed bothered.

I broke the silence. "Are you okay?"

She ignored me.

I smiled and said, "Don't tell me somebody's jealous?"

"Are you kidding me? No offense, but you're not my type." She laughed and then turned up the radio.

After she dissed me, I kept silent because I was a little embarrassed.

* * *

The next day, I woke up early and caught the bus to my grandmother's house. She lived in the slums of Opa-Locka. Death angels haunted the streets in the form of drive-bys in most neighborhoods. Regardless of a crime-infested city, I had a praying grandmother.

When I got to her front porch, the smell of fried fish permeated the air. I knocked on the door, anticipating a plate of cooked food. My cousin Nicky peeped out the window and shouted, "Who is it?" as if she had an attitude.

"Jermaine."

Nicky was my oldest cousin. She was a pretty girl, but four kids had taken a toll on her body. Although she was twenty, she looked thirty. My other cousin, Tasha, was in eighth grade. She seemed next in line because she was hot in the ass too.

Nicky opened the door and then sat back down on the couch, braiding my cousin's hair.

"Where's Granny?" I said, closing the door.

"Girl, if you don't hold yo' head straight I'ma beat cho ass!" she said.

I felt bad for my 5-year-old cousin as she sat on the floor crying with a snotty nose. "Don't fuss at her like that, girl," I said.

"When yo' ass get some kids then you can tell me how to raise mine." Nicky always seemed mad at the world because she had four kids and three no-good baby daddies.

I walked through the house and it was a mess; the kids had junk everywhere. My grandpa was sitting in his wheelchair sleeping. He had Alzheimer's and colon cancer.

My Uncle Pete stepped out of the kitchen with flour on his hands. "'Ey there, boy."

"What's good, Uncle Pete? You got it smelling good up in here, bro," I said.

Uncle Pete sniffed the air then imitated Michael Jackson. "Hee-hee!" he said, moon walking back into the kitchen. Sometimes, he acted like he didn't have 'em all. He was another one who couldn't seem to get it together. Uncle Pete had a drug problem but he was cool whenever he wasn't smoking dope.

I grabbed a piece of fish out of the kitchen. Then I knocked on my grandmother's bedroom door. "Come in," she said. When she saw me, her face lit up. I was her favorite grandchild because I had my head on straight.

I sat at the foot of her bed and we talked. I let her know the deal with Roy, and she welcomed me with open arms, even though she only had three bedrooms.

"You know this is home, too, baby," she said.

"Where am I gonna put my things?"

"Don't worry. Your uncle has space in his room. Hopefully, he'll be outta my house in a month or two."

"What about Tasha and them? Do you think they'll mind?"

"Don't mind them. Half the time they're running the streets."

"I'll be back with my things in the morning, okay?"

"I'll be waiting on you."

Before I left, my grandmother gave me a sweet potato pie. I almost ate the whole thing on the bus ride home.

* * *

By the time I'd ridden three buses en route to Coach Baxter's house, it was nighttime. I hopped off the bus with my basketball and half a pie. Then I darted across a busy highway and started walking up the block to Coach's house, which was four blocks away. I put on my headphones while I walked the neighborhood. A couple of minutes later, a police car eased up alongside of me. Two white police officers were in the car. The heavy one told me to stop, and then got out of the car. He had a hand on his gun as if I was a suspect.

I was asked for ID but I only had a bus pass.

"Sit down!" he said.

I put my things down and sat on the ground.

The other officer got out of the car and watched. "Where are you headed?" he said.

"My coach lives in the neighborhood."

"You don't really expect us to believe that, do you? What's your name, boy?" the heavy one said.

After I gave him my name, he got in the car while his partner stood on post. "I didn't do nothing wrong," I said, shaking my head.

After sitting on the ground for fifteen minutes, the heavy officer got back out of the car. "Get your ass up," he said.

I got up and looked at him.

"Don't you dare look me in the eye like you got a fucking problem, nigger." He picked up the pie off the ground and dumped it into the middle of the street. "Eat it or I'm taking you to jail," he said.

"Come on, why are you doing this?" the other officer said.

"You shut your fucking mouth!" he yelled, turning red in the face.

The heavy officer had me with my back against the wall. I didn't wanna go to jail or get my ass beat. I'd witnessed enough dirty cops handing out fake charges and beating cats down for fighting back. I kneeled down and started eating the pie while he got a kick out of watching me.

After I ate the pie, they got in the car and sped off. Hate and anger filled me as I threw rocks at their car.

Fifteen minutes later, I made it home. I rang the doorbell and Lindsey opened the door. I walked past her without speaking.

"How rude," she said.

I couldn't care less what she or anyone else in the house thought of me. I was ready to pack my things and go. The morning couldn't come fast enough.

Ethan came running up to me and showed me his new Xbox video game. I put on a fake smile and walked to the guest bedroom. Before I could get in the room, Coach stopped me.

"Dinner is ready," he said.

I snapped. "I'm not hungry."

"Are you okay?"

I wiped the sweat from my forehead. "I'm good."

"Then come join us for dinner. We're having your favorite: Popeyes. Go wash up."

I went in the bathroom and got cleaned up. Then I ate dinner. Everyone was jolly good, while I was silent. No one could get a sound out of me because I had shut down.

After dinner, I showered and got ready for bed. Ethan begged me to play Call of Duty: Black Ops with him. Even though I had ill feelings towards white folks at the moment, I couldn't take it out on him. I followed him upstairs to his room. We passed Lindsey's bedroom and she was listening to "Grenade" by Bruno Mars, as she lay in bed talking on the phone. I took a second glance because her thighs were nice. Lindsey caught me and smiled.

Ethan and I played the video game until it was time for him to go to bed. I marched back downstairs to go to bed also. Lindsey cut the corner and bumped into me, spilling her juice on the floor. "Holy shit, you scared the crap out of me," she said.

"Sorry." The juice dripped off my hands.

"Here, I'll get you a paper towel." She grabbed some paper towels out of the kitchen and handed me a couple.

"Thank you." I wiped off my hands and then knelt down to help her clean up the spill.

Lindsey stood up. "You know my friend really thinks you're hot."

"Your friend isn't my type," I said, wiping the floor spotless.

"What is your type?"

A chick with a big booty and a small waistline, I was thinking. "Smart and sexy," I said, rising from the floor. I towered over her petite five-foot-five frame like a giant.

We looked into each other's eyes and started laughing.

"Oh my gosh, you're so tall," she said.

"Oh my gosh, you're so short," I said, mocking her Valley Girl accent.

After the laughter stopped, we got quiet. I licked my lips because I was at a loss for words.

Lindsey stood on tiptoes and kissed me. Just then, we heard a noise and took off in opposite directions.

* * *

For a week, I put off going to live with my grandmother. Lindsey had a brother on pause. We had fun together, like hanging out and going to the movies. But I'd promised my mother I would go, so I finally did. The first two weeks was hell. I dreaded living with my two loud-mouthed ghetto cousins. Living with my grandmother was tough. Every day there was drama: Tasha and I didn't click because she had a nasty attitude for a little girl; my other cousin, Nicky, had crazy baby daddies that were possessive; my uncle was back to his old ways – stealing to buy drugs; the kids were bad as hell; Pops was in and out of the hospital battling cancer . . . and the list went on. I needed peace. It was too much going on in my grandmother's house. Every night, I dreamed of a peaceful place to call my home.

After practice one night, I caught the bus and walked the rest of the way home. Every day I'd get home around ten o'clock. Walking the streets at night was like walking through a jungle; wannabe-thugs and drug dealers owned every block. Everybody knew me but no one bothered me. They knew I didn't have nothing but a dream. I was too poor to rob. At times, I was offered money because cats felt sorry for me.

When I made it to my block, I saw Chance sitting on the back of his pop's Eldorado pickup truck. My new pal looked out for me. If I needed change, he gave it to me in exchange for small favors like watching his dogs. He and his pops made plenty of money fighting dogs.

Chance's blue nose pit bull started barking as it saw me coming down the street. I stopped in my tracks because she was vicious. I'd seen her rip other dogs to pieces. I thought it was sick and I didn't see the enjoyment in fighting dogs. "'Ey, yo, get your dog!" I said.

Chance put the dog inside of the house and then came back out the door. "I need a favor," he said.

"What's up, bro?"

"We need you to keep an eye on the dogs for a couple days. Red has a big fight in Ocala."

"No problem."

"You know we'll break you off."

* * *

Friday night, Chance and his pops got back in town. They had two wounded dogs on the back of the truck. I watched them beat the dogs out of their misery with a shovel and then bury them in the backyard. It was brutal. I collected my money and left.

Saturday afternoon, I hit the mall with Kevin and White Chocolate. I had two hundred dollars in my pocket and I was ready to spend it. I needed new clothes and shoes. Two hundred dollars didn't stretch far at all. I saw a lot of nice things but I couldn't afford them. White Chocolate bought a fresh pair of Lebron's out of Footlocker while Kevin and I window-shopped.

Walking out of the Footlocker, I spotted Lindsey working at a kiosk selling hot irons. After her customer left, I walked up and spoke hello. She smiled and gave me a hug as if we'd known each other for years. I introduced her to my homies. When I mentioned she was Coach's daughter, their whole body language changed. They gave her two thumbs up and walked away.

I stayed and chatted with her for a few minutes.

"What are you doing tonight?" she said.

"Chilling." I took off my cap and looked in the mirror. I was long overdue for a haircut but I was out of luck because I had spent my last bit of change on Sbarros' pizza. "I need a haircut bad," I said.

Lindsey felt my rough hair. "I like it," she said, looking into my eyes through the mirror.

I put my cap back on.

"You should come over; my folks are out of town for the week-end."

"Oh yeah?"

Five minutes later, my homies came back. "Let's go," Kevin said.

"I'll see you tonight," I said to Lindsey.

"Okay," she smiled.

After we walked away, my homeboy started teasing me. "Coach is going to kick you off the team," White Chocolate grinned.

"We're only friends. Ain't no harm in that, is it?"

"Did you smash?" he said.

"What part don't you understand about the word friends?"

"She is kind of fine for a white girl," Kevin said, looking back.

White Chocolate got offended. "What do you mean for a white girl? Don't go there because I can give you a whole list of hot chicks."

"Why you getting mad? It's not my fault white girls don't have no ass."

"Jessica Simpson," White Chocolate said.

Kevin burst out laughing. "Psyche yo' berry!"

White Chocolate kept throwing out weak names.

"Give it up," Kevin teased him.

"Kim Kardashian."

"Oh now she can get it."

"Y'all are nuts," I said.

I showed up to Lindsey's house at 7:30. I rang the doorbell five times before she opened the door.

"Sorry, I was upstairs," she said.

"That's okay." I waved goodbye to Kevin, and then walked inside and sat on the couch. The phone rang and Lindsey disappeared upstairs, as I watched a full episode of *Everybody Hates Chris*.

Thirty minutes later, Lindsey came back into the living room and led me upstairs. She kissed me at the top of the stairway.

I placed my hands on her hips and pulled her close to me. My nature had risen. "Your father would kill me if he knew I had my hands on you."

"Don't tell me you're a chicken shit?"

"I ain't no chicken."

She giggled. "Then come on, silly," she said, pulling me into her bedroom.

We laid on the bed and started kissing. Lindsey's hands crept into my boxers while mine crept into her panties. We felt each other down as our clothes hit the floor. The contour of her breasts and hips was perfect. Filled with emotions, I looked into her light brown eyes. "You sure you wanna do this?" I said, rubbing her hips.

She kissed me and said, "Yes."

I ripped open the condom in my back pocket, put it on, and slid home.

That evening after we had sex, we kicked it all weekend long. Lindsey was wild. Every second of the day, she was all over me. I could tell that she was hooked because she couldn't keep her hands off me.

Kevin picked me up before her peeps got back in town. He drilled me with questions. "Did you smash?"

"You know I don't kiss and tell."

Kevin laughed and gave me high five. "Is she a keeper?"

"Nah, bro, I don't have time for distractions. I'm trying to ball this year." I meant it too. The last time I had a girlfriend was freshman year. Our relationship didn't last because basketball always came first.

"Hustle!" Coach yelled at practice.

I ran back on defense to defend the two-on-one fast break. Chris tried to dish the ball across the lane and I tipped it. The tip led to an easy score on the other end.

"Way to get back on defense!" Coach said, stepping on the court. "Let's wrap it up, guys."

Everybody huddled as Coach hyped us up for our first home game tomorrow night. We were all pumped up.

"Listen up, men – one team, one goal: The state title!" Coach said.

On game night, I had a clean low-cut fade. White Chocolate had shaved his head bald. I thought it was funny because he looked like a skinhead. As we prepared to leave the locker room, I scribbled my father's initials on my new kicks. Wearing his initials on my shoes was a ritual.

The #1 graced my back as our team filed into a packed gym. The voice of T.I. blazed the gym during warm-ups. I was in a zone before the game. Al though I had a lot of pressure on me, I felt confident.

A smile spread across my face when Momma walked in the gym with my two little sisters. They waved at me and I waved back. Having their support meant a lot to me.

At tip-off, we won the jump ball. I dribbled the ball up court and ran a play. The ball got swung back to me and I hit a short jumper from the corner.

"Woot there it is!" the crowd shouted.

It felt good to break the ice. I got back on defense and slid my feet. We got a steal and the ball was outlet to me. I led a three-on-one fast break and dished the ball to Chris off a no-look pass. He took it to the house on a highflying dunk.

Everybody jumped out of their seats. "Woot there it is!" they shouted.

All game long, we had our way. I couldn't be guarded as I constantly slashed to the basket for two. They switched to a zone but White Chocolate was on fire with the three ball. We made them pick their poison. I couldn't wait to see the box score as coach emptied the bench.

The final score was 87-51. I thought our squad looked good. In the locker room, Coach congratulated us on an excellent win, and he made us believe that we were a great team.

When I walked out of the locker room, my mother was standing in the hall. I gave her a big hug. "Hey, Momma."

She smiled at me. "My baby was awesome tonight," she said.

"What can I say? Your boy ain't no joke."

Sasha smiled at me shyly.

"Ain't that right, pretty girl?" I said.

"Yup," she giggled.

White Chocolate patted me on the shoulder as he walked by. "Good game, J."

I leaned against the wall and looked at my mother. She seemed sad. "What's wrong, Momma?"

"I want you home."

I shook my head. "I'm okay. You got to let me be a man."

"Do you need any money?"

"I said I'm good."

"Alright, I'm not going to force the issue."

"Thank you," I said, kissing her on the cheek.

That night, I slept good, knowing I'd had a good game. My stats were solid; I led the team with 26 points, 5 assists, and 8 rebounds. The rest of the starters scored in double digits too. I was excited about my team and what we could accomplish this year.

During practice the next day, everyone's true colors had begun to show. There weren't enough basketballs to go around. I was fuming because I wasn't getting no shots. Chris was chucking up everything. "Man, pass the fucking ball!" I shouted.

"Fuck you! It ain't your team."

"I am the team, Tito!"

"You ain't nothin' but a ball hog, nigga!"

I pushed him and a fight broke out between us. Everybody pulled us apart as we squabbled on the floor. Coach kicked us out of the gym and made us go home. I released my anger out on the garbage can sitting in the hallway. After I'd kicked it, trash blew everywhere.

The following day, Coach called me into his office and decided to bench me for Thursday's game. I thought he took it overboard with his John Donne quote: 'No Man is an island, entire of itself; every man is a piece of the continent.' I got the message, but his choice to bench me made me furious. I thought of quitting the team. After he told me I couldn't play, I decided not to show up for practice that week.

On game night, Coach got bold and told me I couldn't sit the bench. "What?" I said, while we stood face-to-face in the locker room.

"You're welcome to enjoy the game from the stands."

"You can't do this to me, Coach. There's gonna be scouts out there," I begged.

He folded his arms like he didn't care. "You made the choice not to be apart of the team, Parker."

"Whatever, I'm out; I don't have time for this shit!" I said, punching a locker. I went home heated. After thinking it over, I had decided to quit.

For a week straight, I got home before five o' clock. That was new for me. I didn't know what to do with myself because I was used to playing ball. It was apparent the team missed me. Thursday night's game, I watched them get their butts kicked. After all that running off at the mouth, Chris had more fouls than points. It was hard watching the action from the stands. White Chocolate had begged me to come back but I was waiting for Coach to reach out to me.

One day after school, I passed the gym. White Chocolate stopped me. "J, we need you. It's not the same team without you. Why don't you come back?" he said.

"Coach Baxter can kiss my ass. I'll transfer before I play for him."

He gripped my shoulder. "You need to put your personal differences aside. You and I worked too hard for this. Forget the haters." He gave me five and then walked in the gym.

I gave it some thought on the way home. When I got off the bus, a cold breeze hit my face. The start of winter was around the corner and I could feel it in the air. My lips took a beating as I headed up the block.

Louie hit the corner and rolled down his window. Nia was sitting on the passenger's side, looking fly. I looked at her and she turned away.

"Hey, amigo. Need a ride?" Louie said, laughing at me.

"Nah I'm good."

"You sure. It's cold and your lips are chapped."

"You got jokes for a dude who can barely speak English."

"She likes my accent," he said, pointing at Nia.

Nia eased up on him. "I sure do, Daddy."

I stopped and looked at Louie. "What do you want?"

He laughed. "Take it easy, hombre. I sense hospitality in your voice, eh?"

"You mean hostility," I said, shaking my head.

"Would you like a job?"

"I'm cool."

"No?"

"No. What part don't you understand?"

Louie flashed a stack of Benjamins in front of my face. "Come on, I can use a little help on the block. "Call me," he said, handing me his number.

"Alright, Louie," I said, shaking his hand. After we chatted, he let up his window and sped off. Even though the money was enticing, I thought about Momma. I ripped up his number and let it blow in the wind.

That night, I lay awake in bed thinking about my decision to quit the team. The situation was bothering me like the funk in my uncle's bedroom. Sex was in the air. Almost every night my uncle had a girl in his bed. He was forty-two and the girls he smashed always looked fifteen or younger. I thought it was a shame that a grown man like himself enjoyed sleeping with little girls.

As my uncle bounced the girl on his lap in enjoyment, he panted. I stared at the moonlight, wishing I had a positive male role model in my family. After a while, I got tired of the noises and slept on the living room couch. That was until Nicky came home from the club and made me sleep on the floor.

7

———

GAME FOUR – I WAS in attendance. We looked pitiful. Bones spotted me in the stands and joined me to watch the game. "Why aren'tchu on the court?" he said.

"I got into it with the coach."

"For what?"

"I don't even wanna talk about it, bro."

"You too good to be sittin' up here in the stands."

"Oh well. If they need me, they know where to find me."

It was tough being a spectator. We were getting manhandled, 64-31. White Chocolate got dunked on and the home crowd went ballistic. I pulled my cap over my face in embarrassment. Coach Baxter looked frustrated as he paced the floor looking for someone to go to on the bench.

Fourth quarter, I left the gym after Chris got his shot blocked into the fifth row of the bleachers. I'd had enough. Me and my dudes chilled outside until it was time for me to go. "Won'tchu come chill at the crib with us? We gon' call up some hoes and get it crackin'," Bones said.

Floyd flashed a bag of weed in front of my face. "Lookie lookie," he grinned.

I wasn't up for kicking it. "Y'all go 'head. I'll catch up with you cats later," I said.

* * *

At 10:50, I headed to the bus stop to catch the 11:15 bus. My bus pulled up in less than five minutes. I showed the driver my bus pass then headed toward an empty seat in the back. It was the only seat available. The bus driver pulled to the next stop and picked up more people. It was super crowded on a Friday night. An old lady swayed across the aisle as she made her way to the back of the bus. No one budged. I helped her and gave up my seat. A big smile spread across her face. "Thank you, young man."

"You're welcome."

I put on my headphones and eased into my own world. J. Cole was on blast while I chilled. Slowly the bus began to empty. I grabbed a seat up front and kicked back comfortably. One by one people began to disappear. I stared out the window as we drove the city. The city lights lit up the night. A few people walked the streets in their heavy coats trying to keep warm. A Bentley pulled up to the red light alongside the bus. I almost broke my neck to see who was in it. A brother who resembled Chad Ocho Cinco was behind the wheel. I could only dream that car was mine.

When we pulled up to the next stop, there was a man digging inside the garbage can as if he was searching for gold. I watched him open a McDonald's bag and shove food inside his mouth. It dawned on me that he was the same bum that I had run into at the park. Suddenly, his words *you only get one shot* began to playback in my head. I pictured myself digging in a garbage can for food. The whole episode made me face reality quickly.

The next morning, I found myself at Coach's front doorstep. I rang the doorbell and he opened the door. He looked shocked to see me. The first thing I did was apologize for popping up to his house at ten in the morning. I felt small while I stood in the cold hoping for his sympathy. He took a sip of his coffee and invited me in.

I sat down in the living room and waited for him to return. I heard Lindsey's voice from the kitchen. She walked out of the kitchen and headed upstairs when I caught her attention. She had on a midriff top and a pair of skimpy shorts, looking sexy. I nodded hello. Lindsey took a loud deep breath as if she was upset with me. Coach walked out of the kitchen and we looked away from each other. I hated that I didn't get the opportunity to plead my case before she headed upstairs to her room.

Coach Baxter sat down across from me. I didn't even know where to begin.

"Well?" he said

I looked him in the eye. "Coach, I wanna play."

He set down his coffee mug. "Why should I let you back on the team? Give me one good reason."

"'Cause I'm sorry for letting everybody down . . ." I started rambling but I meant every word I said. " . . . I'm willing to do whatever it takes to earn my spot back on the team. I made a mistake and I learned firsthand there ain't no satisfaction in being a quitter."

"Sounds like you've punished yourself enough." Coach stood up and put his hand on my shoulder. "I'll see you at practice on Monday."

I wanted to jump for joy.

* * *

Monday, I was at practice. It felt good to walk across the gym's shiny hardwood floor. I made amends with the squad. Everybody seemed cool, even Chris. We squashed the beef and played ball. There was no feeling greater than being back on the court.

Friday's game, we played away. Coach had chosen to make me come off the bench. I was cool with it. At a record of 1-4, I was hoping someone would step up their game tonight. I cheered on my team from the bench even though I hadn't stepped foot on the court through the entire first half. We were getting blown out. The sea of black faces in the stands clowned us. Coach grabbed me after White Chocolate blew an easy layup. I walked over to the scorer's table and waited. We were down eighteen points. It didn't look like we could climb back in it. No one was hustling.

The buzzer sounded for substitutions.

I worked my way into the game by playing hard on defense. My first two points came off a steal. My adrenalin was pumping. I wanted to win. Our sixteen-point deficit meant nothing to me. I hustled like the score was tied. A couple of times, I cleaned the floor diving for loose balls. If we were gonna lose, I wasn't gonna let us go out without a fight. We went on a 10-0 run. Everyone in the gym had to pick up their faces off the floor. I hit a three, cutting the lead to three points.

The other team called a time out.

"It's my time!" I shouted at the crowd. All the life had been sucked out of the building. It was completely silent as we gathered on the sideline. Coach's face was full of intensity in the huddle. I felt a hand on my shoulder.

White Chocolate looked at me and said, "Let's go, baby! We're in this thing."

We walked out to the floor with 1:20 left in the game. Six-Nine handed me the ball after pulling down his tenth board of the night. Everyone stood up as time ticked away on a thriller. I brought the ball up court. The second I saw an opening I took it. I slashed to the basket for two. The opposing coach eyed me down the court as I wagged my tongue.

"It's over!" I shouted at him.

Down one point, we snagged another defensive rebound. It seemed like everyone was holding their breath as I dribbled the ball up court. With time ticking away, I drove the ball and got fouled.

"That's bullshit! I ain't touch him, Ref!" the cat guarding me shouted.

"Stop crying and play ball, sissy," I said.

He got up in my face. "Keep talking shit, bitch!"

I head butted him. "You better watch your mouth, pussy."

The ref stepped between us and threatened to call a tech. I stepped to the free throw line and hit both shots to put us in the lead. The other team called a time out.

The crowd was dead.

Chris grabbed me. "Yeah, boy! That's what I'm talkin'bout!" he shouted in my ear.

After the time out, we held them scoreless on the series. I pushed the ball up court. The double team came. Chris broke free on the right wing and I hit him for a spot-up jumper. The crowd sat down after he sunk it. I sprinted up court banging on my chest.

Time ran out while the other team threw up a pair of desperation threes and missed. Our squad walked off the court teasing the crowd. Everybody booed us. One hater threw a cup of water at me. Two of my teammates held me back because I was ready to fight. I let it go because victory was the sweetest revenge. For the first time in weeks, we filed out the gym as winners.

* * *

Our winning streak continued for weeks. My name lived in the paper as I averaged 29 points, 6 assists, and 8 rebounds per game. College scouts flocked to our games to watch me play. At a record of 21-4, I had my team positioned in first place in our division. Everybody had jumped on the bandwagon. Sold-out gyms became common for our squad as the press raved about me. The drug dealers would come and bet money on our games. Louie would give me a hundred bucks for each slam-dunk. I stayed fly in new clothes, and I kept a fresh haircut. I enjoyed every bit of the hype. In school, I was the man. The girls would do anything for me: give me rides, give me money, and offer me sex.

After practice one day, I got in the car with Ashley. She drove me across town to my grandmother's house. Nicky and her boyfriend were in the front yard making a scene.

"Thanks for the ride, cutie," I said, getting out.

Ashley smiled. "No problem. See you later."

I waved as she drove off.

Nicky's boyfriend shoved her against the car. I was gonna let it slide until he smashed her head against the car window. I threw down my bag and bum-rushed him. I scooped him up and slammed him in the dirt. He got up swinging. We were outside throwing fists like two boxers in a ring. I hit him in the grill and he stumbled back to the ground. "Hit a man, punk!" I yelled, standing over him.

He got up and ran to his car.

"No, Deion!" Nicky screamed. She pushed me in the house. "Go, Jermaine, please!"

Her boyfriend grabbed his pistol. I took off through the front door. He popped one at me, but the bullet missed my head by an inch. My heart was racing as I lay on the living room floor scared to breathe. My grandpa sat in his wheelchair staring at me like I was crazy. Three more bullets pierced the door. I crawled in the kitchen begging God to spare my life. Suddenly, the shooting ceased then I heard a car peel out.

Nicky ran in the house looking for me. "Jermaine!" she cried.

"I'm in here," I grimaced in pain.

She looked in the kitchen and found me on the floor "Oh my God, are you okay, Cousin?"

I looked down and saw blood on the floor.

Nicky started screaming. "You're shot!" She picked up the phone and called 911. The ambulance took forever to get to my grandmother's house.

8

I LAY IN JACKSON MEMORIAL Hospital. A bullet had grazed my shoulder. The nurse stitched up the wound and placed a bandage over it. Coach Baxter heard the news and called me. I explained everything to him. Coach felt bad and offered to take me in if I needed a place to stay. Just then, my mother rushed into the ER to see me. She was hysterical; I thought she was gonna have a heart attack.

I hung up with Coach. "Calm down, Momma, I'm alright," I said.

Momma was shaking as she held me close. "Please come home, Jermaine," she cried.

I couldn't go back home. I would've rather slept on the streets than to live under the same roof as my stepfather.

"I don't want you back at Nana's house."

"I have a place to go."

"Where?"

"I'm gonna stay with my coach again."

"Jermaine, you can't live with those people. You have a family."

"They're good peoples and they'll look out for me."

After I was released from the hospital, I showed up at Coach's doorstep late that night. Momma backed out the driveway upset. I felt like a bum as I carried three hefty garbage bags inside of

Coach's house. It was hard going through the changes but I accepted the hand that I was dealt.

Coach led me to the guest room and it seemed like déjà vu.

* * *

The next two days, I went to school with a chip on my shoulder. I was drained because I hadn't slept in two days. My business was in the papers, negating me the right to privacy.

One night during a game, I almost let it get to me. I was very emotional throughout the contest. I played like I was on a mission, scoring a career-high 52 points.

After the game, I hopped in the car with Coach. I laid back and relaxed on the passenger's side. Coach reached over and handed me an AT&T packaged cell phone.

"A gift for me?" I said.

"I'm sure you could use it, right?"

I smiled. "Thank you."

He smiled back at me. "No problem. I have great news for you."

"Good news for me? Is that possible?"

"Several schools are interested in you."

I sat up straight. "Really?"

"Don't act so surprised."

"Several schools like?"

"UM, Syracuse, Michigan, North Carolina . . . just to name a few."

"Wow!" I wanted to turn a back flip.

Coach smiled at me. "If you keep producing you'll have every Division I school in the nation knocking at your door. Have you considered taking the SAT or ACT?"

I sat back and caught my breath. "No."

"We have to get you prepared. This summer I want you to take the ACT."

"Okay," I nodded.

Despite being homeless, I felt good.

When I got to the crib, I laid across bed and called my mother.

"I'm surprised you thought enough of me to call," she said.

"Momma, please stop trying to make me feel guilty."

"Where are you calling me from this time? A payphone?"

"I got a new cell phone."

"Oh?"

"Yes, ma'am. My coach gave it to me."

She got silent for a brief second. "I really wish you were home . . . everybody misses you."

I cut her off. "Momma, guess what?"

"What?"

"I have a lot of colleges interested in me."

She screamed. "I'm so proud of you, Jermaine! You better go 'head on, baby."

"I am. You're gonna be proud of me one day."

"I'm already proud of you." She started singing, "My baby going to college . . ."

I laughed.

Someone knocked at the door. "Hold on, Momma," I said, opening the door.

Lindsey handed me a set of clean towels. "Welcome back."

I winked and said, "Thanks."

Late in the middle of the night, I felt soft lips on my neck. I turned and Lindsey was smiling over my shoulder. She had turned me on.

"What are you doing in here?" I whispered.

"Relax, everyone is sleeping."

"You locked the door?"

"Yes," she grinned, showing her pearly-whites. "Do you miss me?"

"Of course I do."

"Then how come you never called?"

"Long story."

"I'm listening."

I wasn't in the mood for talking as I lay in bed on stiff. I grabbed Lindsey's hips and pulled them on top of me. Lindsey started making noises as she bounced on top of me like a trampoline.

"Shhh," I said, giving it to her good.

After smashing it, I moved her to the side and exploded.

Lindsey kissed me on the lips and then got up. "Bye," she said, tiptoeing out the door.

"Deuces."

Two nights later, Lindsey snuck into my room again. She crawled under the covers and stole my heart. That night we made our relationship official.

* * *

Saturday afternoon, we played Lindsey's school, Gulliver Prep. The gym was filled with preppy white folks cheering on their team. Lindsey shouted my name from the stands. I played it cool as she and her friends watched me during warm-ups. A scout from the University of Florida was in the stands watching too. I became a bit nervous because I wanted to do well. UF was my favorite school because of Coach Donovan; he was a winner.

At the start of the game, the Raiders had come out shooting lights out. They weren't an athletic team but they hurt us on the pick-and-roll. Once we buckled down on defense, all the cheering subsided. Good defense turned into good offense. I got into a rhythm and was knocking down shots everywhere on the floor. On one series down the floor, I caught an alley-oop from White Chocolate and then turned my ear up to the crowd. I couldn't hear a sound except for Lindsey's clique cheering us on.

By the fourth quarter, we were up 97-54. I had scorched the Raiders for 39 points, 5 assists, and 8 rebounds. Coach emptied the bench. I had a good time watching my team finish off the game. Chris and I sat the bench rolling.

After last weekend's game, our record stood at 28-4. The district playoffs were two weeks away. After a rough start, we were favorites to win a division title. The press deemed me as potentially the number-one point guard in the state.

One day at school, I was approached in the parking lot while walking to the car with Ashley. A clean-cut, spiky-haired man jumped out of a BMW and stopped me. He looked to be in his mid-forties. "How are you, Mr. Parker?" he said.

"I'm good."

"The name's Scott," he said, shaking my hand. "Headed to lunch?"

"Yep."

"Can I talk to you?"

"I didn't do it."

He smiled. "Ah ha, I see you have a great sense of humor."

I looked at Ashley and told her to go ahead to McDonalds without me. "Just bring me back a number two with a Sprite."

"Okay." She got in the car and went on her way.

"This better be real important, man."

Scott told me to hop in his ride.

"Nah, that's alright I'm good," I said.

"Come on, I don't bite. I'm here to help you."

"Help me?"

"Hop in and let's talk."

I got in on the passenger's side. It sounded like he was out to help himself. Scott talked a good game. He was an NBA agent interested in representing me. I thought he was jiving.

"You're definitely NBA material. If it weren't for the age rule you'd be well on your way in next year's draft. I'm going to keep my eye on you . . ." He handed me his card. "Let's keep in touch."

"Most definitely."

"It was nice meeting you and one day I hope to work for you, Mr. Parker."

I got out of the car feeling as if I was on top of the world.

* * *

Two weeks down the line, we blew out Southside High for the division title. Everybody was hyped up at the thought of bringing home a state title. Most of the pressure was placed on me to help deliver the Bulls its first championship. Each practice,

I could tell Coach wanted it more than anyone on the squad. In preparation for the state title game in Orlando, his late nights were dedicated to watching and breaking down film. He was on edge. I was too.

9

I STOOD AT THE FREE throw line: sweat trickling down my face, heart racing, prepared to seal a victory over Seminole High for the championship. Chris tapped me on the rear after I made the first free throw to put us in the lead with 0.6 seconds left in the game. On the second attempt, Coach instructed me to miss it to run out the clock. The ball bounced off the rim, sealing the game. At the sound of the buzzer, the bench and our fans rushed out to the floor. We had pulled off an upset against last year's undefeated State Champions. Last year's Gatorade National Player of the Year was shut down; I'd held Brandon Williams to 11 points.

I grabbed him at the neck of his jersey. "Keep your head up, bro," I said.

He walked away, ignoring me. The rest of his team showed good sportsmanship. One of them hugged me. "You balled tonight. I gotta give it to you, dawg. Congratulations."

"Thanks, bro. I appreciate it."

After the game, the media attacked me in the hallway. There were a bunch of cameras and mics shoved in my face. "Jermaine, how does it feel to deliver Northwest High its first state title?"

Unshy of the spotlight, I looked at the reporter. "No man is an island. It took teamwork and everyone stepped up tonight . . . . I'm proud of these guys," I said, shoving Chris as he walked past us.

White Chocolate tossed me a towel and I wiped the dripping sweat off my face.

"Thanks, man," I said.

"How did you manage to hold Brandon Williams to a season-low eleven points?" an aggressive female reporter shoved a recording device to my lips.

"All year long coach stressed defense. As a team we bought into his system and it paid off."

"Looking at your stats tonight 31 points, 5 assists, and 9 rebounds, is there anything you can't do out there?" another female reporter fought her way to the forefront.

"No," I said confidently.

She smiled. "Great job."

"Thank you," I said, walking away from the press.

We celebrated in the locker room like a bunch of fools. I had to pinch myself.

* * *

After leading my team to a state title and averaging a career-high 29.5 points, 4.9 assists, and 8 rebounds, I was awarded the Gatorade National Player of the Year. As part of the award, I was given free accommodation and tickets for the ESPY awards in Los Angeles. It was fun flying out to L.A. with my mother. It was the first time she'd ever traveled abroad. It made me feel good to be able to treat her to a nice vacation. During the trip, I got high praise from college coaches and players. I felt like a star those two days in L.A.

After my trip to L.A., life was sweet. My junior year flew while I had the time of my life. I received an invitation to the Elite 100 Basketball Camp in Virginia. The event was for the best high school players with NBA potential. During the four days at camp, I got better. I participated in games and worked with former NBA players and coaches. They helped me elevate my game as I competed against the best high school players in the country. The schooling didn't stop on the court. They gave all the players a lesson on life and peer pressure. It was good stuff because I didn't have a positive black male figure in my life.

When I got back to Miami, Coach Baxter picked me up from the airport. I was tired as I struggled to keep my eyes open on the ride home. I hadn't taken a break off the whole summer and I didn't intend to. Attending the Nike Peach Jam Tournament in South Carolina was next on my agenda.

Coach looked at me. "How did it go?"

"It was a lot of fun."

He handed me a padded envelope. "Surprise."

"What is it?" I said.

"Open it and see."

I ripped open the padded envelope and opened the letter inside. My ACT scores were good; I'd earned a composite score of 26. "Woo hoo! That's what I'm talking about, baby," I shouted.

Coach gave me high five. "The ball is in your court. Now it's all up to you."

I smiled. "Thanks, Coach."

"Don't mention it."

Coach was my hero. I knew if it weren't for him I'd be on the streets instead of the road to college.

1 0

A YEAR LATER, I SAT in class wondering where did time go as I was announced Gatorade National Player of the Year for two consecutive seasons. On top of the honor, Rivals.com and Scout.com had me ranked as the number-one point guard in the nation. Senior year, I'd averaged 31.9 points, 3.5 assists, and 8.3 rebounds per game, earning a spot on the USA Junior National Select Team. Votes to the McDonald's All-American game and a selection to the Jordan Brand Classic were in the bag also. Although my team fell short of a state title, I held my head high. The personal accolades brought a little comfort to defeat.

My face lit up when I was presented with the trophy in class. I took a few pictures and enjoyed the moment. After the hoopla, Ms. Love made us get back to work.

When the bell rang, I handed in my writing assignment. I had become a good writer. My hoop diary reflected it, as I'd give my fans and the media weekly updates of the recruiting process.

Ms. Love looked at me with a big smile on her face while she sat on her desk. "Keep up the good work. You're sitting on an A."

"Thank you."

"Don't thank me. You're the one who put in the time and effort. What are your plans, now that you have a big future ahead of you?" she said, folding her arms proudly.

"I just wanna be successful like you, Ms. Love."

She smiled. "Are you trying to charm me?"

"Is it working?"

"No."

"Darn," I said, snapping my fingers.

"Boy, I'm old enough to be your mother. Get on out of here," she said, whacking me across the head.

White Chocolate waited for me in the hall while I went to the bathroom. A white kid standing at the stall smiled at me. "Congratulations!" he said.

"Thanks." It was amazing that everyone seemed happy for me except for some of my own people. Over the past year, I had gained more enemies than friends. I had a lot of haters. A couple of my teammates like Chris and Six-Nine couldn't stand that I was getting all the attention from big-name schools, while they were hoping for a scholarship.

White Chocolate and I headed towards the cafeteria. As usual, I received mixed stares. Some cats liked me while some disliked me. One way or another I didn't care while I continued to shine.

Ashley stopped me in the hallway upset. "Oh, so you can't answer your phone now?"

"Can you move? I'm on my way to lunch."

She put a hand on her hip and stood in my way. "Why won't you pick up the phone, Jermaine?"

"I've been busy." Ashley and I had done it only one time. Ever since those two weeks ago, I regretted it, because she wouldn't leave me alone. She'd call and text me a hundred times a day. Al though Lindsey was my heart and soul, I'd chosen to test the waters, which had come back to haunt me.

"You weren't too busy while you were trying to get between my legs!" she said, shoving me.

"Shorty, you need to keep your hands to yourself. I'd be wrong if I slapped your ass."

White Chocolate stepped in between us. "Chill," he said.

"It's not all that, Jermaine."

"Then why are you sweating me?"

"I need you."

"You need me?" I laughed in her face and walked away.

White Chocolate shook his head. "These girls don't know when to quit."

"Who you telling, bro? They go psycho after you smash."

After lunch, I went to see Coach. After all this time, I still lived with him. He'd taken me in like a son. When I walked into his office, he gave me a big hug.

"I'm proud of you, kid," he said.

"Thank you." I set my trophy on his desk and sat down. "You could've told me they were gonna surprise me."

"Then it wouldn't have been a surprise." He sat down at his desk and handed me a roster for the McDonald's All-American game. The thought of playing in the All-American game had me beaming. I couldn't wait to ball on national TV.

During our meeting, Coach enlightened me on the discussion that he and my mother had had with a college recruiter a week ago. "Still undecided, huh?" he said.

I took a deep breath. "Yeah, Coach. It's tough."

"Take your time. There's no rush. You have to do whatever you think is best. Never mind what anyone else thinks or has to say. It's your decision."

I had narrowed my top ten choices down to five: Duke, Kansas, Kentucky, Syracuse, and UF. Letters from college students and alumni flooded Momma's mailbox in attempts to persuade me to commit to their schools. Coach had guided me through the process of choosing schools that were best suited for me. The beginning of the year, I had visited Kentucky. I thought they had an excellent basketball program; they had a solid reputation for developing point guards and sending them to the pros. Indecision had me stuck in limbo because everyone was pulling at me. The pressure to sign with the best school was a stressful process.

When I got home, I admired my trophy for a few seconds. Then I put it out of sight and out of mind. I sat it in my closet and kicked off my shoes. I had new boxes of kicks stacked high.

Expensive shoes were one of the gifts I received from sponsors on a regular basis. I had more pairs of Jordans than Footlocker.

My cell phone rang while I got undressed. I let it ring as calls poured in from different people. When I saw Lindsey's number, I picked up the phone. "What's up, baby cakes?" I said. Our relationship was good even though we had to keep it a secret around her folks. They would've never approved of us dating underneath their roof.

"Open the door," Lindsey said.

I hid behind the door butt naked as she walked into the room and locked the door. "Uh, can I help you?" I said, covering my package with two hands.

She relaxed on the bed. "Don't mind me."

I hopped in and out the shower. Lindsey watched me pull out clothes for Kevin's party.

"Something's on your mind?" I said.

She started twiddling her fingers nervously. "Umm, kind of."

"Let it out or forever hold your peace. I slid on a pair of jeans when she whispered underneath her breath, "I'm pregnant."

"Say what?"

"I said I'm pregnant."

It felt like my whole world had crashed. I wasn't prepared to be a father. "No way, girl. I thought you were on the pill?" I said, pacing the room.

She became flustered. "It's not all my fault, okay!"

"You're right; it's my fault too. I'm sorry. I'll give you the money for the abortion."

"No."

I stopped pacing and looked at her. "What do you mean no?"

"I'm having the baby."

"Are you out of your mind, girl? Your father would kill me."

"This has nothing to do with him."

I kneeled down and looked her in the eye. "Listen to me. Now is not the time for a baby. I don't care how you paint the picture – it doesn't look good."

"You're only thinking of yourself, Jermaine."

"No, I'm thinking about us. Trust me."

She shook her head. "I'm having it!"

I covered her mouth. "Shhh before someone hears you."

She swatted my hand away from her mouth. "It's my body."

"Do you really think that's gonna sit well with everyone?" I whispered.

"Who cares?"

"I care. What about my feelings? Do you love me?"

"Yes."

I stood up and pulled her in my arms. "Then consider what it's gonna do to my reputation. You know I would do anything for you, Lindsey."

She started crying.

I wiped the tears from her eyes. "Do it for me, please."

"No!" She pushed me on the bed and walked out of the room.

I watched her stomp up the stairs. Coach walked out of the kitchen, looking curious. I closed the door and sat on the bed frustrated.

Kevin called and I picked up. "What time are you coming?" he said.

"Man, I don't think I'm coming."

"What's wrong, J?"

"Lindsey's pregnant."

"Oh shit! Coach Baxter is gonna fuck you up. What are you gon' do?"

"I don't know but I'll call you back later."

I hung up and called my mother because I was upset. When I told her, she wanted to drive across town and strangle me.

"How many times have I told you to wrap it up? Have you lost your mind?"

"It was a mistake."

"I'm sure it was a mistake, but you have to keep that thing in your pants. You should already be hip to the game . . . and just to think she's got you wrapped around her finger now. The thought of it makes me sick. I feel like driving over there and choking the bitch!"

"Momma, calm down. That's why I can't talk to you about anything because you always get mad."

"You damn right. She's not the right one for you. There are plenty of beautiful, intelligent black girls in the world and you choose to impregnate a white gal. I don't know what's gotten into you, child."

I was tired of Momma always throwing color into the equation. "Momma, please don't go there right now because color doesn't have anything to do with it."

"Oh, I'ma take it there because if you were any other Joe Blow off the street, she wouldn't want you."

I sighed. "That's the thing, Momma, she's been there for me before all of this."

"Child, please, if you had any good sense you would listen to me . . ."

I put down the phone because I couldn't take it no more.

* * *

Late that night, I ended up going to Kevin's party. I had to get out the house.

Floyd and I rolled up in his Taurus. Everybody was at Kevin's party. The block was lined up with cars. There were a lot of cuties on the scene. Of course, the haters were out too. I spotted a whole bunch of them.

Floyd and I got out of the car and checked out the party. The DJ had "Rojer That" by Young Money on blast while everybody got loose. It was hot as bodies jammed packed the house. The girls noticed me right off the bat while I stood in the cut.

Nia ran over and hugged me. "Hey, boo," she said, kissing me on the cheek.

"What's up, shorty?"

Floyd gave Nia two thumbs up while her back was turned. I shook my head and gave her two thumbs down. After Nia unleashed her tight hold on me, she tipped away for a drink.

My homie took a sip from his cup. "Tell me you wouldn't wife her?"

"Negative."

He felt my head. "You must be sick!"

When Nia came back, Floyd couldn't keep his eyes off her body. His tongue wagged out of his mouth as she bounced her booty to the music. I on the other hand, didn't pay her any attention while I thought of fathering a child. Through the night, I wore a fake smile while people clamored around me.

Bones walked over and wrapped his arm around my shoulder. "Oh, shit, what's up, fool?"

"What it do, bro?"

He lit a joint and took a puff. "Ooh woo!" he said, smiling. Everyone seemed happy while I was miserable at the moment. "You okay?" he said.

"He's been tripping all night," Kevin said.

"I'm good, yo," I said.

Bones threw his hands in the air when Wiz Khalifa's album was put into rotation. Nia started grinding up against me.

"Will you chill out?" I said, pushing her away. She got mad and left because I wouldn't give her the time of day.

"Loosen up, J. You can't let that situation keep you down. You gotta stay strong. Feel me?" Kevin shouted over the music.

"Yeah you're right."

"Everything happens for a reason."

Bones passed me the joint. "This whatchu need right here, boy."

I took a puff and coughed because it was strong. "Whoa!" On the next puff, I took it slow. After puffing weed, it relaxed me. I had a couple of drinks and enjoyed the rest of the night.

As I walked out the door, I brushed shoulders with Nicky's boyfriend named Deion.

"Look at this shit," he said, stepping to me. He had an entourage, as he talked tough. "I thought I put a bullet in yo' punk ass . . ."

"Look, I don't want no trouble."

Deion hit me in the mouth and I retaliated with a fist to his face, creating chaos in the house. Everyone scattered as the fight moved from inside the house to the front yard. I had Deion on the ground beating his face in. One of his partners struck me in the back of the head and I fell over, clutching my head. My homies ate him up like a pack of piranhas. A one-on-one fight had turned into a street brawl. Within five minutes, the police hit the block and everyone ran. Floyd helped me to the car and I got in. Bones and an unknown person hopped in the car too. Bones was in the back seat fuming as Floyd sped off. He slung his dreads and shouted, "Dawg, them motherfuckers don't wanna see us!"

The bald dark-skinned dude sitting in the back seat was amped up too. "They done fucked with the wrong one now!" he said.

"One of them got me good," I said, feeling the knot on the back of my head.

"Let me see," Floyd said.

"Nah, I'm good."

"Don't worry. I split him like boo-yah!" Bones said, smashing a fist into his palm.

"You bleeding," Floyd said, hitting on the light.

Blood was dripping from my head

"You gotta get that stitched up," the bald dude said.

Bones handed me a towel and then pulled a pistol from his waist. "No, forget that shit. Let's go get them fools!"

"I'm with you, cuz," the bald dude said.

"Put that gun away before you shoot somebody," Floyd said. Then he introduced me to his peoples. The dude was named Luther and he seemed like a soldier.

"I got yo' back, cuz," he said.

I started feeling lightheaded and my words became slurred.

"We gotta get cuz to a hospital."

Floyd drove me to the hospital against my wishes. I wanted to toughen it out like a man. My homies sat and waited for me the whole night. I had given the hospital a fake name because I didn't want my business in the papers. While I was in the ER waiting to be helped, one of my mother's girlfriends recognized me.

"Are you all right, sugar?" Mrs. Katie said.

"Yes, ma'am."

She glanced at the bloody towel covering the back of my head. "It doesn't look like it. How long have you been waiting?"

"About an hour and a half."

"Oh, no way!" She started raising hell.

A nurse came over to assist me. She gave me an IV and a doctor stitched me up. I thanked Mrs. Katie because I probably would've bled to death.

When I walked out the ER, it was 5:45 a.m. My homies were in the waiting area sleeping. I tapped Floyd on the shoulder and he woke up.

"You straight?" he said, staring at my bandage.

"Yeah," I said, grimacing.

"Damn 'bout time, fool," Bones said, stretching and yawning. "We thought they had put you on ice."

When I walked outside, I was able to get phone reception. I had a load of missed calls. Lindsey had left me a voice message crying that she would have the abortion. At that moment, I knew there was a God. "Thank you, Jesus," I said.

That morning, I crashed at Floyd's crib. Then I returned home at six o'clock. Lindsey opened the door and let me in. "Where the hell were you? Everyone was worried."

"I'm okay. Where's Mr. Baxter?"

"He's out with Mom. What happened to your head?" she said, following me down the hall.

"I don't wanna talk about it." I walked into my room and sat on the bed. "Can you get me some ice, please?"

Lindsey ran to the kitchen and brought me some ice.

I placed a towel of ice over my head. "Thank you," I said.

"Did you get my message?"

"Yes."

"Well, what do have to say about it?"

"I'll give you the money."

"I don't get a hug, a kiss, or a thank you?"

I set the ice on the dresser and pulled her into my arms. "Thank you so much, baby."

The Baxter's pulled into the driveway and Lindsey scrammed. I closed the door and peeled off the bandage on my head. I didn't want Coach inquiring about the bandage. Five minutes later, someone knocked at the door. I opened it and Coach came in.

"Is everything all right?" he said.

"Yes, sir."

"You didn't come home last night."

"I stayed at a friend's house."

"I understand but next time pick up the phone and give us a call."

"I'm sorry."

"No pun intended," he smiled and walked out of the room, closing the door.

As soon as he left, my phone rang. I grabbed it out my pocket and said, "Hello."

Momma started raising hell; Mrs. Katie had told her that she saw me in the ER. Momma had found out about the fight at the party too. "Do you want to end up in jail? It's a lot of talented brothers in jail, you know."

I sighed. "No, I don't wanna end up in jail."

"Then what is your problem?"

"I don't have a problem. I did what I had to do."

"Sometimes it takes a bigger man to walk away."

"Like I said: I did what I had to do."

"No, here's what you need to do! You need to get rid of all those so-called friends of yours and get focused. You've come too far to let some thugs ruin it."

I took a deep breath. "See there you go jumping to conclusions. They didn't have anything to do with it."

"That's not the point! Lord knows, I'll be happy when you go off to college . . . .."

"Momma, I have to go."

"You hang up on me if you want to – I will come over there and show out."

I sat and listened to Momma preach for an hour. Everything she said went into one ear and out the other. I felt like the Fresh Prince because Momma didn't understand.

* * *

After a week and a half, the lump disappeared and the stitches were removed. But the conflict between Deion and I was deep rooted. Supposedly he'd put a hit out on me. I wasn't the least bit worried because I had peeps that had my back.

Late one night, I snuck upstairs to check on Lindsey. She had had the abortion and was dealing with depression. My heart pounded as I made way into her bedroom like a smooth criminal. "Hey," I whispered, locking the door.

She didn't reply.

I walked over to the bed and shook her awake. "How are you feeling?" I said.

"Leave me alone," she said, turning her back to me.

I got underneath the covers and wrapped my arms around her body. "Do you still love me?"

"Yes."

"Turn around and tell me."

"No," she sniffled.

I rubbed my hands through her hair. "Don't be mad at me. I really feel like we did the right thing." Suddenly, I felt guilty for forcing her to have an abortion. "Will you please look at me?"

Lindsey wouldn't look at me.

At that point all the toughness inside of me had hit the door. I got emotional. "I'm sorry for making you get rid of the baby. I will never put you through that again . . .." As I lay there pouring out my feelings, she let go of her anger and resentment towards me.

Lindsey wrapped her arms around me and cried, "I love you."

11

Two MONTHS LATER, I BALLED at the McDonald's All-American game in Columbus, Ohio. I was named co-MVP alongside Brandon Williams after posting 26 points. Brandon had thirty-one; he was a tough 6'2" point guard who reminded me of OKC's Russell Westbrook.

We stepped to the middle of the court and shared the spotlight for the award. Brandon and I embraced each other out of respect. "Aye, good game, man. You the real deal, boy," he said.

"I appreciate that, bro."

We turned and smiled for the cameras. It was a dream come true to play on primetime television and shine in front of NBA scouts.

A day after the game, a fast-talking agent approached me. Every night he'd made it his business to camp outside the hotel. On my out of the hotel to head back home, he was in the lobby checking out.

"How's it going, Jermaine?" he said, rushing over to me.

"Good."

"Can I talk to you for a second?"

"I don't have much time."

"I'll make it quick." He congratulated me on last night's game and my performance at the Nike Hoop Summit in Portland, two weeks ago. "You should let ASG Sports Agency represent you. You have the potential to be a high pick in next's year's draft." He was a hundred light years ahead of me. The NBA draft hadn't crossed my mind considering I hadn't even chosen a college to attend. "The Alliance Sports Group is a powerhouse, Jermaine. The same lucrative deals we've negotiated for great players like Rajon Rondo, O.J. Mayo, Brandon Roy . . . we can make happen for you."

"Nah, I'm good, bro." I got on the team bus like I didn't hear him. All week I'd been hearing the same blasé from different agents. Scott had warned me. At times, it was overwhelming because everyone talked a good game.

As we rode to the airport, my cell phone rang constantly. Incoming calls from family and friends poured in. Balling on ESPN network had initiated the frenzy. I received a couple of calls from college coaches who were on my radar for signing day. They congratulated me on a good game. I was on a call with the head coach of Kansas for thirty minutes. He had me excited as he emphasized the great basketball player I could become under his coaching staff. Every coach I'd talked to made my decision tougher during the recruiting process. Al though I'd agreed to make my decision following the Jordan Classic in three weeks, I was still undecided.

After we hung up, I called Lindsey because I hadn't heard her voice in a day. She seemed excited to hear from me.

"What are you doing?" I said.

"I'm going to work out. My hips are spreading. It's disgusting."

"Please don't go anorexic on me. I like curves. Did you watch my game last night?"

"No."

"That's not cool at all."

"Sorry, I fell asleep."

"No excuse." My phone beeped. "Hold on," I said. I clicked over and it was Scott.

He congratulated me on a good game.

"Thank you," I said.

"You're awesome, Jermaine! You have NBA scouts drooling at the mouth . . ."

Lindsey hung up as I listened to Scott soup me up. I felt like hanging up on him because he was annoying.

"The ball is in your court now!" he said.

After we hung up, I called Lindsey back. "Sorry," I said.

"I'll talk to you later."

"Why?"

"I'm going running."

"Call me back. I should be at the airport by three this afternoon."

"I love you."

"I love you too."

When I arrived at Miami International Airport, I received bad news from Momma. She was upset because the bank had issued a foreclosure notice on the house due to unpaid taxes. Her and Roy owed $9,500 in back taxes. "I don't know what to do," she cried.

It hurt me to hear Momma cry. "What did Roy say?"

"He's sick about it but what can we do at this point? Nothing but let the bank foreclose on the house."

"No, we can't let them take the house."

"We don't have a choice."

I grabbed my luggage from baggage claim. Then I headed outside and waited on Lindsey. She pulled up in less than five minutes. I threw my luggage in the car and got in. "I'll get up the money," I said, kissing Lindsey on the cheek.

"No, Jermaine, I don't want you getting into no trouble."

"I'll call you back, okay?"

"Did you hear me?"

"Yes, I heard you."

I hung up the phone upset. I didn't want Momma to lose the house and I had no idea of where I was gonna get ninety-five hundred dollars. Listening to my mother, I could tell she was desperate – and desperate times called for desperate measures. Bones came to mind but then I doubted he had that kind of cash flow. The situation had me aggravated.

Lindsey waved at me. "Earth to Jermaine," she said

"Sorry, I was just thinking."

"About?"

I turned down her Katy Perry CD because it was driving me nuts. "You wouldn't understand."

"You never give me a chance."

"'Cause you can't relate to a lot of things I go through."

"Don't you dare pass judgment on me."

"It's true. You don't know what it's like to struggle. Your parents have everything and y'all live all carefree like *The Brady Bunch*."

"You're so wrong."

"Stop fronting, yo. It's not working, okay." I called Bones and asked him for the big favor. He claimed he didn't have it, although he always fronted like his money was long.

"Got dang it," I said.

"Sorry, dawg, I just handed my baby mama ten stacks to get a car . . ."

Yeah right, I thought.

"The only other person I know with that kind of cash flow on hand is Louie," he said.

"Yeah, but I don't know if he's cool like that, bro."

"He's cool. Besides ninety-five hundred dollars ain't squat to him."

"Tell me something I don't know. He had work for me at one time. I wish I'd hooked up with him when I had a chance. My mother wouldn't be going through this crap."

"You can't cry over spilled milk. Hit him up. It's never too late."

"Yeah, I think I'm gonna do that, bro."

"The only problem: I ain't seen him around in a minute. You know cats get ghost when their name come under suspicion."

"Don't tell me that, Bones."

"I know where his peoples stay. His aunt lives in Little Havana."

"I need you to swing me over there later on."

"No problem. Call me."

"I'll talk to you later." I hung up and slammed my phone on the dashboard.

Lindsey jumped. "Jermaine, what's wrong? Talk to me please!"

"I need ninety-five hundred dollars. There you have it, happy now?"

"Holy shit! For what?"

"The taxes are due on my mother's house."

"What are you going to do?"

"I'm gonna do whatever I have to do to make sure my family doesn't get thrown out on the streets."

* * *

Later that evening, Bones and I took a stroll through Little Havana. The sound and sight of Cuban culture manifested itself through vibrant colors and loud music. Festive colors lit up the town like a bright candle in a dark room. I felt like I was in Cuba.

Bones and I knocked on Louie's auntie's apartment door. A lady yelled, "¿Quién es?"

Bones and I looked at each other speechless. The woman peeped out the door, and then quickly closed it back as if she was afraid. Bones knocked again and she started yelling, "¡Vete!" at the top of her lungs.

"Let's go before she calls the cops," I said, feeling uneasy.

We ran and hopped back in the car. "What now?" Bones said.

"Let's take a ride over to Louie's peeps restaurant."

We rode to Milly's Restaurant but Louie's family told us he was in Santo Domingo.

"Whatchu gon' do?" Bones said, cranking up the car.

I shrugged and stared out the window hopeless. I hated the thought of not being able to help Momma. She and Roy had done everything they could do, too, from what she'd told me.

Out of the blue, Scott called to make sure I'd made it back in town safe. It felt like the heavens opened when he said, "Let me know if you need anything."

I took a deep breath. "I need a big favor if you don't mind."

"Sure what is it?"

"My mother's house is in the process of going into foreclosure. I need a loan for ninety-five hundred dollars."

"Why don't you come by so we can talk?"

Suddenly a frown had turned into a smile. Scott gave me directions to his home in Fort Lauderdale. We hit I-95 and headed north to downtown Fort Lauderdale. He lived in a waterfront mansion on Las Olas Isle. The size of all the homes in the area was ridiculous. They couldn't have sold for less than ten million. It was hard to believe that people lived so lavishly, while others struggled to make ends meet.

Bones' eyes were the size of saucers as we entered through a security gate, which surrounded Scott's multi-million dollar mansion. "This don't make no sense," he said.

"Tell me about it." Seeing Scott's home made me dream. "One day my pad is gonna be this big," I said.

When I rang the doorbell, Scott opened the door. "Welcome, gentlemen," he said.

We walked in and paused at the front door, fascinated.

"Come on," he said, leading the way.

I got sick at the sight of a thirty-foot ceiling and a life-sized balcony. I felt as though I had walked through the pearly gates of heaven. Onyx marble and Italian porcelain covered the countertops and floors.

We sat in a huge living room with a wide-open view of the Intracoastal. Scott offered us drinks and made us feel comfortable. After a couple of minutes, he handed Bones the TV remote and took me out back. He had a private yacht anchored outside of his house.

I sat down and stared at the mansions along the waterfront.

Scott took a seat and smiled. "Let's get down to business shall we."

I rubbed a hand across my head. "Your house is bananas."

"You can say I've done quite well for a Michigan State graduate."

"Who you telling?" I nodded.

"So have you considered foregoing the NBA draft next year?"

"No."

"I think you should seriously think about it."

"I don't know what the future holds. What if I'm not drafted?"

"Hopefully you will be. I'm willing to take a chance, are you?"

"Damn right."

He laughed. "I promise you'll be pleased with my agency. The proof is here," he said, handing me a full list of his clients. "Not bad, huh?"

I was impressed with the star-studded list. "Not at all."

"So, what do you say?"

"You got a deal."

He laughed. "Where do you think you're headed for school?"

"I don't know yet but I'm leaning towards Kentucky."

"Not a bad choice."

"But then my heart is telling me UF."

"Go with your gut feeling." He wrote a check for $9,500 and handed it to me. "Is that all you need?"

"I'm good. It should cover my mother's taxes."

"Don't be so modest. He ripped up the check and wrote another one for $10,000. "Buy yourself something nice with the rest."

My eyes grew gigantic when I saw multiple zeros. Without hesitation, I verbally agreed to let Scott's agency represent me. I felt as though I had committed to something worthwhile. I prayed it didn't come back to haunt me though.

Scott hugged me and then shook my hand. "I'm counting on you. I wouldn't do this if I didn't believe in you," he said, looking me in the eye.

"I won't let you down, Scott."

12

COACH BAXTER AND MOMMA SAT beside me during the press conference held at school to announce my decision. I had chosen the University of Florida. After a few trips to Gainesville at the beginning of the year, I was impressed with their program. A good night in the town impressed me too, but Momma had a lot to do with my final decision. She had convinced me to stay closer to home instead of packing up for Kentucky. They almost had me though.

After I signed the dotted line, I hugged Momma and gave her a big kiss. It was a special day for my family and I. At the same time, it was a bit overwhelming. All the cameras and questions thrown in my face had me a bit nervous.

"What triggered your final decision?" one of the reporters asked me.

"I felt comfortable with the situation at Florida and I believed I could get better ..."

"With the loss of three key players to graduation and the potential of two underclassmen bolting early for the NBA, how do you see yourself fitting into a starting role?"

I looked at the ESPN reporter. "I'm confident in my ability to play at the college level. I know it's not gonna be easy but with the support of a great coaching staff I feel like the sky's the limit."

"We know that you possess the skill and size to play at two positions on the floor. Would you rather play on or off the ball?"

"I'm willing to do whatever it takes to win."

The questions kept coming and some of them were irrelevant.

"How long do you plan on staying at Florida? Have you had any thoughts of entering the draft?"

"That's not something I've thought about. I have my mind focused on the present moment ..."

Less than a week after I'd made my decision, I was chosen to grace the cover of *Slam* magazine, alongside Georgia's top high school recruit, Dwayne Thomas. I struck a pose in the forefront with the basketball at my waist for next's month's June issue. I was labeled as college basketball's next big star. The more hype I got, the more expectations I was demanded to meet.

* * *

After graduation, I prepared for Gainesville. I made my rounds and visited close friends and family. Lindsey had let me use her ride to take care of business. I had to go see my main man, Doug. I sat at the county jail happy to be on the other side of the law. Doug's case was part of an ongoing fight between the state attorney and the prosecutor. The prosecutor working the case wanted to see my homie behind bars for life.

Doug walked out slowly. He looked surprised to see me as he reached for the phone.

The mood was somber.

"What's good?" I said

"Nothing. I thought you forgot about me."

"Not at all."

"So what's going on, Mr. Big Shot?"

"Life, you know. What's going on with you?"

He set a hand on top of his head "They tryin' to give a brotha life. If I could do it all over again I would be on the other side of the glass window. It ain't no fun in here. But I'ma ride this thing out on faith. Hopefully by 2020 I'll be eligible for parole."

I shook my head because that was a long time away.

"I'm just glad you didn't forget about me. Some of us get all Hollywood and forget where we've come from, you know?"

"You know me – I'm gonna always keep it hood."

"I luh ya, bruh."

I saw the pain in his blood red eyes. "I love you too, bro."

Visiting Doug was tough. I walked out of Dade County Jail heavy-hearted. On my way out the lobby area, I was stopped. A well-dressed man carrying a briefcase stood in my way. "Hey, you're Jermaine Parker," he said, stroking a hand through his fluffy hair.

"Yes."

He smiled and shook my hand. "Incredible. Nice to meet you!" Then he started talking basketball. All of a sudden, everybody caught wave of who I was. I became encircled by several of his colleagues. They were excited. An overweight police officer stopped and stared as if he was in shock. Then it struck me that he was the dirty cop who harassed me one night. I wanted to beat his ass, but the look on his face was far more priceless.

When I walked away from the crowd, he still stared at me with a startled look on his face. I gave him the finger and kept walking.

* * *

That same day, I dropped in on my mother. She fixed me a good home-cooked meal. It felt strange coming back home and sitting at the dinner table. I missed it. Like the nights Momma would throw down in the kitchen and make the best smothered pork chops in the world.

Roy walked in the house while Momma and I were laughing about the time she caught me with a girl in my room when we were supposed to be in school. She beat the brakes off me.

Roy spoke good evening to us.

I hadn't talked to him since I'd left home a year and a half ago. "What's up, Roy?" I said.

"Man-to-man, you know I really appreciate what you did. If you ever need a place to come this is your home."

I wished he wouldn't have wasted his breath because I didn't do it for him. If it were left up to me he would've been on the streets.

He unbuttoned his Pep Boys' uniform shirt and started talking to me as if we were down like four flat tires. "I was telling my buddies at work how much your game has improved since freshman year. I mean, I always knew you had it in you. A lotta the guys at work don't believe you're my son." He started laughing loudly. "You should swing by and surprise everybody if you're not too busy."

Momma smiled.

I stood up to leave. "I'm always busy."

Suddenly the room got quiet.

"Oh . . . maybe another time then," he said.

"Yeah, maybe."

Roy took off his shirt and walked in his bedroom.

Momma looked sad. "Jermaine, don't be so cold. Everyone makes mistakes."

"He'll be alright." I hugged Momma and walked to the front door. My sister smiled at me. "I see you, pretty girl," I said

"Jermaine, call me," Momma said.

"Alright. Love y'all."

I got in the car and drove over to Kevin's house. He was nursing a bad knee. Over the past six months he had put on a lot of weight. I felt bad for him because no colleges wanted to offer him a scholarship. He seemed angry as we sat in his mother's living room watching TV.

"You alright, bro?" I said.

"Hell no. I'm tired of sitting around here doing nothing with my life."

"Give it time, Smitty."

"These schools are dirty. They wanna use you and then when you get hurt, they stop calling. That's why you gotta use them, too, and charge it to the game."

"Damn right."

Kevin flipped the channel to ESPN. College football announcer, Brad Nessler, was giving his take on the most impressive teams in the Big Ten Conference. Kevin was burning up when Michigan State became the topic. Kevin had made a verbal commitment to play for their program but they showed no interest after he tore his ACL last fall. "I don't know what I'm gon' do," he said.

"Don't quit."

Kevin's mother shouted his name from her bedroom. He took a deep breath. "Every day she gets on my nerves."

"You gotta take it easy, bro. It's gonna be alright."

"That's easy for you to say when you got the world eating outta the palm of your hands."

"I didn't come over here for you to make me feel guilty."

"My bad."

"Nah, I'm good, bro."

He hobbled out of the room on crutches.

ESPN switched gears and started talking college basketball. When my name was mentioned, I tuned in hard. My picture was on TV as different announcers gave their analysis of me. My decision not to sign with Kentucky fueled negativity but I didn't care. Opinions were like assholes – everybody had one. Shoot, I had to do what made me happy.

"Playing at Kentucky would've been a better choice for this kid," the sports announcer said. "Kentucky's dribble-drive-style offense would've complemented his skills at best. I think he received bad advice from a lot of people. Everyone mark my words, his game will never get to that next level like a Derrick Rose or John Wall . . ."

"I'm going to have to agree with you. Kentucky is known for honing elite point guards into the NBA . . ."

Kevin hobbled back in the room and sat down. I turned the television to 106 & Park. Nicki Minaj was on the famous couch looking amazing. Kevin and I were deeply tuned into the television set until the end. Then we reminisced about the good old times at Northwest High.

* * *

After making my runs, I lay in bed thinking about my life. I felt like I had the world at my feet.

Lindsey knocked on the door and asked for her car keys. She had on a short mini dress and a pair of high heel stilettos.

"They're on the dresser. Where you going looking all fly?" I said.

"To pick up Heidi then we're heading to South Beach. Wanna come?"

"No, y'all go 'head and have fun."

"Please go out with us."

"Uh uh, no."

She grabbed my arms. "Pretty please with a cherry on top."

"Ooh, that sounds good," I said, pulling her on top of me.

"Stop, I have to go." She stood up and fixed her clothes. "Are you coming or not?"

"If you let me hop in the shower."

"Okay, hurry."

I hopped in and out of the shower. Then I got real nice for the club.

We ended up at Club Space in downtown Miami. The joint was live with three different rooms to party. Each room had huge dance floors and they were all packed. We partied in the Techno Loft. Everybody was moving and jumping to the sound of House Music. I felt like I was in a trance as colorful strobe lights beamed the floor in fast motion. Most of the women on the floor were half-naked with fake boobs. It was fun to watch.

I stood on the dance floor while Lindsey went to get a drink. A blond-haired girl flaunted her big breasts in my face and asked if I wanted to dance. I looked at her chest and said, "Nah, I'm good."

After the blond had approached me, a few addicts walked up to me next, asking if I had any drugs. "Hell nah," I said, brushing them away.

Finally, Lindsey came back and handed me a drink. It was good and strong. She put her arms around my neck and started dancing. I stood and watched her shake it like Shakira.

That night, we didn't walk out the club till 3:30 a.m. A big-nosed Italian-looking guy approached Lindsey while we walked to the car. The dude looked as if he had plenty of money. He came on to my girl and disregarded me.

I felt disrespected. "Hey, man, you need to fall back," I said, grabbing her close to me.

He got slick at the mouth. "What does that mean? Is that the new street lingo? Where'd you pick up this homo?" he said, grabbing Lindsey's arm.

I pushed him and he tripped, falling down into the middle of the street. He clutched the back of his head as if he was dying.

In less than a minute, I was sitting in the back seat of a police car.

13

I WAS BOOKED AT THE Miami Police Department and charged with disorderly conduct. I sat in jail angry. Luther was in the same cell for selling drugs to an undercover police officer. He and I chatted. His future seemed headed down the drain. I was grateful to God because I could've been in Luther's shoes.

Coach Baxter came to bond me out of jail. I was given a court date and then released. By the time the sun came up, the incident that happened at the club was all over the news. I wanted to crawl under a rock while the media portrayed me as a monster.

I took it to heart.

That afternoon, I lay in bed upset over the incident. I hadn't gotten any rest. Momma called me throwing a temper tantrum. "That white girl is kryptonite!" she yelled through the phone.

"Momma, don't start!" I raised my voice.

"I'm sorry." She got silent.

I knew I had hurt her feelings but I didn't think it was her business who I'd chosen to be with. Although I disliked Roy, I respected her decision to be with the loser.

Lindsey came in the room. She sat on the bed and started rubbing my head.

"Stop," I said, brushing her hand away.

She started crying.

After I hung up with my mother, I got up.

"Why are you treating me this way?" Lindsey said, drowning in tears.

"Leave me alone. I'm not in the mood, yo."

She stood up and tried to hug me.

I pushed her away. "Didn't I say don't fucking touch me?"

"Jermaine, I'm sorry please don't do this to me."

I shook my head and pushed her out the room.

She banged on the door. "I'm sorry. I love you!"

A couple of days after my arrest, I appeared in court before a judge. I was charged with a misdemeanor and forced to pay a court fine. After that, I apologized for my conduct. My statement was released to the press. I'd made a promise to everyone that I would keep my name clear of trouble.

14

THREE WEEKS LATER, I GOT settled in Gainesville. I lived in a small 2-bed dorm. During the summer at UF, I got acquainted with most of the players and made myself familiar with the campus. My classes were boring. I enjoyed everything outside of going to class like the wild parties and the girls, who would do anything for me. I felt like I was in paradise.

When the fall came, it was a different atmosphere. The classrooms were fuller and the dorms were filled to capacity. My roommate, Devin Higgins, was cool. He was a six-foot, dark-skinned dude with mad handles, recruited out of Texas. The only problem I had was that he smoked too much weed; his lips were blacker than black but that didn't stop him.

I tried to resist the temptation to smoke marijuana but it was hard. It was around so much that I couldn't help it. Everyone did it. I wasn't a weed head though. Every now and then, I would smoke when I felt under a lot of pressure. At times, I'd put too much pressure on myself to do well. It was hard not to feel the pressure when so many people had set their hopes high on me. Last weekend's Fan Appreciation Day was proof. Thousands of people had filed into the O'Connell center to meet the team and receive autographs. That day, it seemed as if I was the center of attention as the fans embraced us. The hype surrounding me didn't stop there. *Sports Illustrated* had picked me to appear on the cover of *College Preview*, which was due to hit shelves mid-November.

I was in high demand and it was tough. A lot of my friends back at home couldn't accept the fact that I was doing big things. They thought I was changing because I no longer had time for them. I didn't let it faze me while I kept focused on school and basketball.

* * *

During preseason, ESPN ignited more frenzy around me. I averaged 18 points, 4.2 assists, and 5 rebounds in our first two games against the London Leopards and the California All-Stars.

When buzz got around campus that I was a potential NBA star, I couldn't go anywhere without the student body recognizing me. Everywhere I went people wanted me to stop and sign autographs. At times, it got out of hand to the point I'd be late for class. I started wearing headphones and keeping my head down so people wouldn't think I was being rude for ignoring them. Off campus, it was the same. Every day it was getting harder to control the cost of fame. I had a lot of people pulling at me, from top-tier agents to beautiful girls. At times, I took advantage of the star treatment, accepting gifts and money thrown my way. Although it was against NCAA rules, there were things I needed that Momma couldn't provide for me while working a minimum wage job.

* * *

One Tuesday afternoon, I headed to film session. We watched tape on our first opponent of the regular season; Syracuse was coming to town. After breaking down film, it was straight to practice. Practice was always intense. My high school practices couldn't compare to the college level of play. Everyone hustled like their futures depended on it. The intensity was high, day in and day out. Every day at practice, I played determined.

I was determined to be the best and to prove all my detractors wrong.

After practice, I headed to the weight room for a couple of hours. My goal was to keep getting stronger. I was a solid 200 pounds. Over summer workouts, I had reached my goal and put on ten pounds of muscle. I had a lot to prove this season because there were a lot of high expectations placed on me. Everyone expected me to be the driving force behind a national championship.

Momma called me as I was leaving the gym. We talked for a good while. She tended to keep me grounded in the wake of my success. *Don't be no fool. Get your grades* was her motto. As I walked across campus, I was interrupted. A blond, curly-haired girl stopped me. "Oh my gosh, you're Jermaine Parker!" she said. She and her friends were excited.

I put Momma on hold. "What's good, ladies?" I said to them.

"I love you," the blond said, hugging me. She introduced herself to me as Megan.

"Nice to meet you, Megan," I said, looking into her blue eyes. Everyone asked for an autograph while she forced me to take her phone number.

I took it because she was beautiful.

When I got to the dorms at eight o' clock, Devin had a cute chocolate girl in the room. "What's up, peeps?" I said, closing the door.

"That's my man Jermaine Parker," Devin said, pointing at me.

"Hi," she waved.

Devin eased his way close to the girl. "I'm horny."

"You're funny," she said.

"You don't see me laughin'," he said, kissing her on the neck.

She pushed him away. "Stop."

Devin got mad. "Then what the hell you came over here fo'?"

I closed my drawer and looked at them. "Tell him don't be talking to you that way."

"Yeah that's right," she said, rolling her eyes at him.

"You either lay it down or hit the door," Devin said.

I went in the bathroom to take a shower. My body was aching all over. I let the hot water run over me until it ran cold. After a hot twenty-minute shower, I felt good.

When I came out the bathroom, Devin was smashing. He had the girl face down and bent over. The things some of the girls would allow to be done to them was beyond imaginable. The word no never crossed their minds. They were out to get theirs and vice versa. I'd never been exposed to a high level of promiscuity until I got to college.

I got in bed and put on my headphones to avoid the noises. After Devin eased her out the door, he bragged. It was a normal thing for him. Every day, he had girls in and out of the dorms. At times, I felt the pressure to have someone in my bed. It was a macho thing.

I picked up the phone and called Megan because I had to show him up.

When Megan walked through the door, Devin seemed impressed. As we sat in bed talking, he started texting me discreetly. One read: *you better get dem drawers tonight.*

I put my phone aside and begun my mission. By the end of the night, it was a mission accomplished.

* * *

The next evening, Devin and I hit the computer lab to work on our research papers. I watched the girls walk past us and whisper.

"Hi," one said, tapping me on the shoulder.

"Hello."

"I don't mean to be rude but my friend wants to know, are you dating anyone?"

"Nawl, baby, he just crush a lot," Devin said.

"Bro, watch out. Who's your friend?" I said.

She pointed to a chubby dark-skinned girl standing in the back of the room.

"Damn what's her name: Precious?" Devin said.

I nudged him. "Yeah, I'm sorry."

After Miss Matchmaker walked away, I went back to work on an eight-page paper. Within forty-five minutes, a pale-faced boy interrupted me.

"What's going on, dude?" he said.

"What's up?"

"Good luck to you guys on Saturday."

"Thanks, man. We need it."

He started talking of the match-up while I was trying to finish my paper. I felt like my life didn't belong to me. I hardly had any time to myself or time for friends. My relationship with Lindsey was void as with a lot of friendships back at home. Juggling school, basketball, and relationships was impossible. I caught a lot of heat from my homies back at home while I was away. A lot of them shot me down because I no longer picked up the phone. I was officially on a new lease. After all, I had a big future ahead of me if I didn't blow it.

Finally, the boy scrammed when one of the lab workers told him to be quiet. I thanked God. I didn't finish my paper until 2:00 a.m.

When I finally got back to the dorms, I flopped on the bed and went to sleep. Before I knew it, it was time to get up for class. Every day I made it my business to sit in front of the classroom, so I wouldn't get distracted. My grades were good. I maintained a 3.2 grade point average. If I didn't do anything else with my life, I was determined to get my grades.

After class, I called Lindsey because I missed her voice. We had made an agreement to be friends because the long distance thing wasn't working out. "Hey you, what's up?" I said.

"Nothing much."

"So what's good?"

"I'm in school and working part-time."

"I miss you."

"You don't really mean it."

"I swear I do."

"Stop it, you're going to make me cry."

"I need to see you. Is that okay with you?"

"So you can hurt me and tell me that it's over again? No thanks I'll pass."

We hung up without any attempt to make it work. I walked across campus like a sad puppy dog. Coincidentally, I bumped into Megan.

"Hi, Jermaine," she said, hugging me. "Where are you heading?"

I gently pushed her away. "To class. Do you mind?" I put on my headphones and kept walking.

In speech class, I had to do a presentation. A copper-skinned girl named Kimberly was the first person to go. She walked up to the front of the class elegantly dressed. Everyone paused at the sight of a diva. She was fearless in front of the classroom as she fought to keep her bangs out the way.

After her five-minute speech, I volunteered to go next. It was Friday and I wanted to get it out the way. I spoke on my favorite sport of basketball.

When class ended, I approached Kimberly. "What's good?" I said.

"Hi."

"Allow me to personally introduce myself: I'm, Jermaine Parker," I said, reaching out my hand. "You don't mind if I call you Kim, do you?"

"Not at all and it's nice to meet you."

I smiled. "I don't usually do this but can I get your number?"

"Wow."

"Wow, what?"

"I'm surprised you aren't busy chasing after some skinny model-looking white girl."

"See, why are you tripping? Love is color blind."

"Then why does your type always see fit to date or marry a white woman?"

"Hold up. Why are you letting all your steam off on me?"

"I'm sorry but it bothers me that you brothers go running to the arms of a white woman soon as you make it."

"I think you need to get to know me first before you pass judgment. Besides, people can't help who they fall in love with, Miss Thing. I know you're intelligent enough to know that, right?"

"Yes but –"

I cut her off. "Write down your number and stop giving me a hard time."

Kim smiled and gave me her number. "Make sure you use it."

"Will do." I looked at the clock and realized I didn't have time to chat.

* * *

A day later, a sold-out crowd of 12,000 came to watch our first game against Syracuse. It was electrifying to run out of the locker room and witness the spirit of true Gator fans. The place was rocking and my heart was beating fast. The excitement was beyond real. I felt like I was on a big stage as the cameras flashed. During warm-ups, I was pulled to the side for a quick interview. ESPN network cameras were in my face.

"Jermaine, can you describe the anticipation of playing in your first game in front of a sold-out crowd at the O'Connell Center?" the reporter asked.

"It's a dream come true without a doubt. I'm really excited."

"What is your team looking to do to spoil a welcoming visit from the Orangemen?"

"Well, we just wanna go out and play our game at both ends of the floor."

"You have anything you would like to say to the people that are watching at home?"

"Hey, Momma, Grandma, love y'all. Smitty, get better, bro."

I jogged back on the court for warm-ups. Everything still seemed unreal. During player introductions, I chewed the taste out of my gum. When my name was called, I wished my father were in the stands to watch me.

At tip-off, we won the jumpball. The crowd was pumped. I brought the ball up court and passed it. We swung the ball against a tight man-to-man defense. With the shot clock running down, I was given the rock; I beat my man off the dribble and nailed an uncontested shot in the paint.

The place went mad.

After I had hit my first shot, I got on a roll and picked their defense apart. I constantly drove and dished.

During a timeout, Coach looked at me in the huddle. "You're doing a great job of facilitating but I need more offense!" he said.

We returned to the floor down three late in the first half. I took more shots like I was instructed to do. I exploded towards the basket and hit a floater in the lane over a pair of outstretched arms, bringing the lead closer. On our next possession, I hit a three against the zone. The cheers escalated when we took our first lead of the game.

Second half, we came back out confident. Coach looked at us. "Let's finish this half strong, men!" he clapped.

I walked out to the floor. The crowd was hyped. We fed off their enthusiasm and dominated the second half. On a side inbounds play, I cut to the basket and hit a reverse lay-up under the rim. I ran back to the other end of the court shaking my head because I was unstoppable.

We won the game 86-78. I finished with 19 points, 8 assists, 6 rebounds and 3 steals.

In the locker room, the cameras were shoved in my face. I answered the media's questions. Then I left the locker room feeling on top of the world. My cell phone kept ringing. Everyone congratulated me on a good game.

Scott was excited. "Jermaine, you were phenomenal!" He started talking about my future. "You have a great NBA future ahead of you, I promise you."

"I don't think I'm ready; I wanna stay and get my degree."

"Excuse me? Are you kidding me? Once you sign an NBA contract, you can buy a degree if it means that much to you."

"I don't know right now. I'm still undecided."

He took a deep breath and said, "Think about it; the future is now, Jermaine. The New Jersey Nets and the Clippers have you on their wish list as we speak."

"Give me time to think it over."

"It's a no brainer."

"Later, Scott." I hung up.

* * *

After the game, I hit the town with a few friends. We had drinks and ate at the Salty Dog Saloon. The establishment had an age limit, but in this town the word no didn't apply to us.

It was a hefty crowd in the small building. People would stop at our table and congratulate us on a good game. Some of the girls flirted with us and we flirted back. One of my homies invited three cuties to our table. We had a good time laughing and cracking jokes. I had my arm around the shoulders of a big-boobed brunette hottie. "Are those real?" I whispered.

"Touch them and see."

"Oh nah, I'm good."

"Aw, how cute, you're bashful." She pecked me on the cheek.

Our waitress brought back the ticket. "Who's paying?" Mario said. Rio was a user, especially when it came to girls. And they'd fall for it every time. I assumed it was because he was a beige-skinned brother with curly hair and brown eyes.

I looked at the ticket and put it back down. "Heck no."

One of the girls volunteered to pay for the ticket.

"Okay, that'll be good," Mario said.

"It's a wrap," I said. I stood up and reached for my cutie pie. A lot of dudes were staring as I headed out the door with one of the finest girls in the establishment.

"Good game, dude. You were frigging awesome!" a boy said, stopping me.

"Thanks, man," I said and kept walking.

Mario and Ricky shared an apartment. Two of the girls followed us back to the apartment. The one who paid the tab was all over Mario. They left the living room to be in private, while Ricky chilled in the front room with me. He was the no-nonsense type. A lot of things we'd do, he'd make it his business not to get involved because he was so-called saved. Girls threw it at him all the time but he was set in his ways. Ricky was a smooth brown-skinned brother who could get any girl he wanted to, which is the reason I couldn't understand it.

ESPN showed clips of our game, but I wasn't interested while I kissed on a perfect set of round boobs. The girl unzipped my pants and felt on my package. "OMG, it's frigging monstrous," she giggled.

Ricky shook his head and got up. "Y'all need Jesus," he said, leaving the room.

After he left the den, things got wild. Sleeping with different women was becoming a bad habit I couldn't break. I was losing it.

* * *

At the rising of the sun, I did my usual routine: class, practice, and weight training. Then I headed back to the dorms. Scott was in my ear urging me to think about the upcoming NBA draft. "The time is now," he repeated.

"Scott, I appreciate all you've done for me, but I'm not ready to make that move. I think I have a great team here and I want a shot at a national championship."

"Have you lost your mind? Who cares? You don't see Lebron James boasting a national championship ring on his finger."

Almost every day I had to hear it from Scott. I had many other people in my ear telling me the same thing. Although I believed that I could be successful at the next level, I didn't wanna rush into things. Besides, my mother urged me to stay in school. Although she struggled, she wanted me to get a good education.

After I listened to Scott beat me over the head, I called Lindsey. We talked into the late night hour. I was happy when she finally agreed to make a trip to come see me. I needed that one person who could help steer me in the right direction.

15

_____

Four weeks into the season, we sat ranked #3 in the polls. My stock was steadily rising with each game. Over the past six games, I averaged 18.5 points, 5.5 assists, 6 rebounds, and 2 steals. Agents began to come out the woodwork. I stayed ducking and dodging them. They were annoying as they followed me around. Some of them stalked me day and night. There were occasions when I'd bump into them in the restroom. They hid in the bathroom stalls or wherever they could to get to me. Sometimes I hated walking out of the dorms.

I pulled Lindsey close to me as we lay in bed. It was her first night in town. Lindsey smelled so good and felt so warm that I couldn't resist her body. I held her tightly because my bones were freezing cold. The coldness of the night had crept through the window of the dorms, making it impossible to sleep. The heat was on but I was still shivering. November had brought a chill through Gainesville that I couldn't handle.

I started rubbing on Lindsey's thigh. "You feel so warm, girl. Turn over."

She turned over and looked at me.

I kissed her lips and crawled on top. "I love you."

"I love you, too, but I'm not sleeping with you."

"It's that time of the month, huh?"

"No, I'm celibate."

"What is that supposed to mean?"

"It means I'm not having sex."

"You can't be for real. It's not like we haven't already done it before."

"I don't care."

"What are you trying to prove?"

"I'm not trying to prove anything, but I'd like to be considered more than just a pouncing bag. Is that fair?"

"You mean a lot to me." I rubbed my hands through her hair.

"Then you would respect my decision."

I eased off of her body and pulled the covers over me, feeling rejected.

Lindsey turned her back to me and went to sleep.

Over the next two days, it was the same thing. I was horny and upset, but I respected her decision to remain abstinent. As Lindsey and I ate Chinese Food on the floor, I needed her opinion. "Hey, Lindsey?" I said.

"Yes?"

"Do you think I should leave school early for the draft?"

She looked at me and shrugged her shoulders.

I sighed. "Come on, I need you right now. This ain't easy for me. Don't bail out on me."

She set aside her chopsticks and looked at me. "What are the pros and cons?"

"It's so many." I broke it down for her and she advised me to stay in school. "Why?" I said.

"It sounds like you stand more to lose if you leave."

"Technically I do."

"Well, there you have it."

Later on into the night, I lay awake in bed still thinking it over. When I'd asked Coach Baxter for his opinion a week ago, he told me to follow my heart. It was times like these that made me wish I had a father. At least I would've known how to deal with a lot of the pressure that came my way. Every day, I was struggling to make the right decisions in my life. Momma was a big help, but there were some things only a man could teach me.

* * *

When Lindsey left town, I felt like she took a piece of me. Kim filled the void. She had her own apartment, a car, a job, and was one semester away from completing her bachelor's degree in elementary education. I thought she was cool.

While at her apartment, I got a call from Bones.

"What's up, fool?" he said.

"Chilling. What's good, homie?"

"I'm just tryin' to come up in this world."

"I feel you."

"Nobody's heard from you in a long time. I thought we was cool?"

"I've been busy."

"Too busy to call? It's like that now?"

"Never that, bro. You know I got love for my peeps."

"I'ont know what to think. I mean, you up there and don't even call us no more. That ain't cool especially when you know we were tight before all this shit. Now you all Hollywood."

"We're still tight. That's not gonna ever change."

"I hope not because you got a lot of cats thinkin' you've switched out. When you comin' back to the crib?"

"Christmas break."

"That sounds like a plan. You need to come through since you claim you still got love for us. How's college and things?"

"It's cool."

"School ain't for me but I'd definitely go fo' da hoes."

Kim walked across the living room in a sheer black nightgown. Her curves were banging. She went in the kitchen and put something to eat on the stove.

"It's some fine ones, too, bro," I said, nodding.

"I'm jealous."

"'Ey, yo, I'll call you back later. I'm about to eat."

"A'ight."

I crept up behind Kim while she stood in the kitchen over the stove. "What are you making?"

"Left over stir-fry chicken."

"It smells good."

"It is." She gave me a taste.

"Wow," I said, impressed. "You're the first girl I've ever met that can throw down in the kitchen."

"What, you thought a blond blue-eyed Barbie could throw down?" she smirked.

I knew it wouldn't be long before she brought up the past. "First of all, I told you my ex-girlfriend just so happened to be of another race. It's not like I went out on a limb to find a white girlfriend."

"Yeah right, Negro. I know how your kind operates."

"How do we operate?"

"Y'all go out and get the blondest blue-eyed heifer y'all can find to flaunt."

"That's a lie. My mother is a strong black woman, so I have nothing but love for black women."

"Then why would you go and lay up with a white one after all your people have been through? It wasn't that long ago when a black man couldn't look at a white woman, or Lord help if you whistled at one. You'd be hung alive. A black man belongs with a black woman."

"That's your opinion, but you're acting ignorant. Love has no boundaries."

"Love does have boundaries because a blue-eyed white woman isn't gonna fight for you or hold you down when times get rough ..."

I walked out of the kitchen because she was getting on my nerves. Ten minutes later, she handed me a hot plate of food to eat. I set it on the coffee table to let it cool. "I'm not really that hungry," I said.

"Are you mad at me?"

I shrugged.

Kim sat on my lap and placed her arms around my neck. "Don't be mad at me," she said, rubbing my face.

"It's all good. You're free to your own opinion, love. I mean, if that's the way you –"

She kissed me on the lips before I could end my sentence. As we kissed, one thing led to another.

* * *

During film session, I was selected for a random drug test. Two days later, my test results came back negative. Leading into the season, I had kicked the habit that some players couldn't break, like Devin. He was selected last week and tested positive for marijuana use. I felt bad for him. He was suspended indefinitely. I took that as a lesson learned.

Today while at practice, tempers heated up between a teammate and I. Eric and a few other players on the second team thought Coach showed me favoritism. Eric had knocked me to the floor on a play where I'd exploded to the basket for a dunk. I got in his face and he threw an elbow at me. Everybody stepped between us before we started fighting.

Eric looked at me. "Keep on thinking you da man."

"I am the man. Check my stats. "

"Drive through the lane again."

"Oh, I'ma bring it every time; you can believe that. You don't strike no fear in my heart."

Eric stood close to seven feet tall and he was a beast on defense.

Coach started clapping. "Let's play ball."

I pushed Ricky off me. "Let me go."

We got back to work on the court. I drove through the lane and Eric packed my ball, swiping me across the head.

"I warned you one time!" he said.

"That was a fucking foul!" I said, getting up.

Eric shook his head. "Stop crying like a li'l bitch, nigga."

"Man, eff you. Come holler at me when you graduate third string," I said, stepping to him.

The starting center, Yakhouba, pulled me away. "Calm down. Don't let him get in your head."

Practice ended and I headed out of the gym frustrated. I was tired of haters.

The assistant coach put his arm around my shoulder. "Don't ever let anybody take you out of your game. Once Eric got in your head, you lost complete focus."

"I know but you seen him trying to hurt me on purpose."

"You're going to face adversity but it's all about mental toughness. That's what life is about, my friend: the way you handle adversity. Trust me, you will face obstacles but don't ever lose your composure."

After the assistant coach finished talking to me, I headed to the weight room. When I checked my phone, I had ten messages. I ran through them all. Most of them were messages from my homies back home. Bones sounded upset because I never called him back last week. He and everybody else was becoming a pain. My mother's call was the only one I felt obligated to return. Everyone else could go to hell.

"Hey, Momma, I got your message. What's going on?" I said.

"Nothing, I just wanted to hear your voice. You know when I don't hear from you, I get worried."

"Momma, it's only been three days."

"And what's your point?"

"I don't know why you worry so much. I'm handling my biz." I brought up the conversation again of leaving school early for the draft, hoping she had changed her mind.

"Why would you do a stupid thing like that, Jermaine?"

"It's not stupid, Ma, if you stop and take a look at the big picture."

"I still think you should stay in school."

"Momma, if I go pro you won't have to work no more and I can buy you a house."

"Basketball is no guarantee, but if you get your degree you'll be able to make choices. I want you to be able to have options. Look at me, Jermaine. Take it from me, without some type of degree or trade – it's hard."

"Yeah, but if I make it then I'll be able to have more choices like how many houses and cars I want."

"You trying to go broke before you get it."

I laughed.

She laughed too. "Look, baby, no matter what you decide I'm going to support you. You're a man now and you have to make your own decisions and live with them."

I took a deep breath knowing that nothing was guaranteed. After all, I wasn't a fool to think I had it made in the shade. "Alright, Momma, gotta go," I said.

"I love you."

"I love you too, and give Sasha and Tiffany a big hug for me."

"Okay." She hung up.

I called Kevin and asked him the same question. We talked it over for ten minutes. "Man, if I were you, I would go," he said. "You can always go back to school. The worst-case scenario, you end up playing overseas, but you'll still be making bread. That's more than I can say for myself. Either way you look at it, you're lucky."

"I have bad days, too. Don't believe all the hype."

"You know how many people would die to be in your shoes right now? I know once I get back in shape, I'm walking on somebody's team."

"You better, bro, but I'll talk to you later. I gotta hit the weight room."

When we hung up, I called White Chocolate and asked him too. He thought I should stay and make a run for a national championship. "I think it would raise your stock in the draft if you got a few more years of experience in a good system."

Yakhouba gave me five as we passed each other in the doorway of the weight room.

"Good looking out today," I said.

"You know I got your back."

I put my ear back to the phone, "You think so?"

"Without a doubt. How many idiots do we know made the wrong decision and didn't get drafted? They're sitting at home wishing they'd stayed in school."

"True." I respected his opinion because he had his head on straight. White Chocolate was working and going to school at Nova University, studying Psychology.

When we hung up, I thought it over for a minute. I was stuck in indecision, especially when I thought of all the money I could make to help my family.

Ricky crept in the weight room and put me in a chokehold.

"Stop playing, bro," I said.

He let me go and got on a stationary bike. Then he started singing the song on his iPod.

I put on my headphones, too, and started working out.

After forty-five minutes, I was ready to go. Ricky took off his headphones. "Where are you going?" he said.

"To the crib."

"I know you aren't still tripping on what happened at practice?"

I wiped the sweat off my face. "Haters don't faze me."

"Oh that's what I thought." Ricky was like a brother to me; he kept me in check. My homeboy was forgoing his senior year to enter the draft. At six-feet-nine, he was undersized for a power forward, but he put up respective numbers to be considered an NBA prospect. "So why are you skipping out so early?" he said.

"I'm gonna rest and get ready for the game this week."

"You sure you're feeling okay? I sense a little frustration in your vibe."

"I got a few things on my mind."

"You can't leave it bottled up. Pressure will bust a pipe."

"I've been thinking about the draft."

"Really?"

"You seem surprised."

"You think you're ready?"

"Everybody else seems to think so."

"It isn't about what everybody else thinks. It's how you feel."

Mario walked into the weight room and came over. "What it do?" he said.

"About to head out," I said.

"Alright, catch you later." Mario was another one who had plans of leaving early. At shooting guard, he averaged 15 points, 2.9 assists, and 6.9 rebounds per game. Yakhouba and Tyreke were the only two starters guaranteed to return for their senior year.

I packed up and headed out of the weight room. A brother in a suit approached me outside. He reached out his hand and introduced himself. He claimed that he represented the Dwight Black Sporting Agency.

"Man, I'm not interested," I said.

"You really need to let a brother represent you."

"No thanks," I said

"Will you please take my card in case you change your mind?"

I took his business card. After he left, I balled it up and put it in the garbage can. Then I put on my headphones and walked back to the dorms in the freezing cold. Devin had the room lit up with marijuana smoke.

I hurried and set the towel back underneath the door. "Man, you're gonna get us in trouble."

"They can't smell it."

"That's a lie. I smelled that crap in the hallway." I opened the window. "You need to kill it, Devin."

A Spanish hottie walked out of the bathroom. "Hello," she said.

"Hi and what's your name, beautiful?" I said, checking her out. She had a nice womanly physique.

"Marie."

"Nice to meet you." I gave Devin two thumbs up.

He winked.

I grabbed some clothes and then hit the shower. When I walked out of the bathroom, Devin was still getting high. I knew security would be on their way down once they got word. It'd happened one time before and I refused to take the blame. I packed a bag, including my things for the game in a couple of days. All week, ESPN raved about our match-up against Stetson. Although Stetson was a lower-ranked seed, they were favorites to win. I thought it was a slap in the face because our squad had been handling business and we still didn't get any respect. All the talk of an upset had me amped up.

After I finished packing a bag, I threw on my leather coat and headed out the door. "Where you going?" Devin said.

"Don't worry about it. Your ass is gon' get it," I said, closing the door.

I walked outside and called Kim to pick me up. Although it was late, she didn't mind. She popped up in ten minutes.

I got in her car and said, "Thanks for coming."

"You're welcome," she said, kissing me on the lips.

At Kim's apartment, I could get rest and keep out of trouble.

* * *

Thursday night, we arrived at the Edmunds Center and got our butts whipped 89-85. We let the game slip away in the last five minutes of the contest. All game long, we had been up more than fifteen points. The taste of defeat was hard to swallow when we'd had the game wrapped up.

I walked off the court frustrated. A game-high 29 points on the stat sheet didn't mean crap to me considering we had lost. I hated losing with a passion. During the press interview, I bit my nails in anger. One reporter got under my skin. I didn't care to be constantly reminded that we fell apart in the last few minutes of the game.

"Jermaine, can you explain the meltdown this team had late in the second half?"

"We just weren't able to sustain energy. They outplayed us when it mattered most."

"In critical stretches of the game, Mario struggled to find his shot. Can you tell us what may've caused him to struggle late in the game?"

"Maybe his shot selection. I don't know, you'd have to ask him."

"How does this team plan to bounce back from a heart wrenching defeat?"

"We're a resilient team; I think we've shown that all season long. We'll be ready without a doubt."

The bus ride back home was miserable in the wake of defeat. It was a very quiet ride. I put on my headphones and went to sleep.

A day later, Coach worked our butts off at practice. We spent the whole practice working on defense. After watching the embarrassing film, it was well needed. Coach had us bent over in exhaustion through practice. His message was made clear: poor defense was unacceptable.

After a week of several brutal practices, our squad got it together. We won our next three home games in blowout fashion. We were back in stride while we prepared for the Sunshine Classic in Tampa, which was to be hosted over the holiday weekend.

* * *

Thanksgiving week in Tampa turned out to be a disappointment for me. Our first game of the tournament, I sprained my ankle. I didn't let it stop me though. I played on a bad ankle throughout each game of the tournament. Although I wasn't a hundred percent, we defeated #2 Michigan State in the finals. I had a flat performance averaging 11 points, 5 assists, and 4 rebounds per game. Although I didn't put up huge numbers, that didn't stop my phone from ringing off the hook. I entertained the idea of leaving school early, but I had no intentions of doing so.

16

MIDWAY THROUGH THE SCHEDULE OUR record stood at 13-1. During the stretch, I had been named SEC Player of the Week four times. *Sports Illustrated* bit on my success and had me scheduled to be in its main issue for January. I had fun while the headlines praised me.

Our team was destined for a national championship and we shared a special bond especially me, Mario, Ricky, and Tyreke. Those cats didn't hate on me because I was getting all the headlines. Everybody was genuine and it showed on and off court. Declaring for the NBA draft was no longer the focal point in my life, although early entry eligibility was around the corner.

Everyone wanted to know my next move, but at this point in life I wasn't ready to leave school. I enjoyed college life and college ball.

One evening, Mario, Tyreke, and I hit the mall. It was a slow day for business as we window-shopped. One of Tyreke's jump-offs worked at Macy's. She gave them the hookup. Tyreke had a charming effect on the ladies even though he was facially challenged; he was a lemon-colored dude with pimply skin.

I was tempted to grab a couple of things but I changed my mind.

"Man, you better grab you somethin'," Tyreke said.

"I'm good, bro."

"You sure?"

"Yeah."

Mario and Tyreke had picked up a lot of brand-name clothes. I stood at the counter and watched everything total up to $487.76. Tyreke handed the girl sixty dollars for the clothes.

As we left out the mall, security approached us.

Damn, I thought.

All three of us were walked back inside of the store. I knew we were in trouble when I saw two police officers and a store manager walking towards us. They asked us for a receipt for the clothes in the bags. We were nervous especially Tyreke. He had been in trouble a couple of times for fighting with his girlfriend.

Mario handed the store manger over the receipt. She looked at the receipt and it was a wrap. Each of us were handcuffed and taken to separate rooms for questioning. My lips were sealed because I refused to incriminate anybody.

That evening, all three of us ended up taking a ride downtown. I sat in the back seat of a police car staring out the window. My head was spinning like a merry-go-round. All I thought about was Momma finding out.

17

THE INCIDENT THAT OCCURRED AT the mall flooded the local news stations and ESPN. We took a thrashing from the media. Security had released the tape to the media to make matters worse. The tape showed Mario and Tyreke shoplifting while I was seldom seen at the register. I got off without being charged while they took the rap. Tyreke was suspended for three games. On the other hand, Mario and I only got a slap on the wrist. After a meeting with Coach, I'd planned to make better decisions. I felt like my future depended on it.

As I lay in bed at Kim's apartment, Momma called me. She was irate. "If y'all feel the need to steal then y'all need jobs!" she shouted through the phone.

"We're not allowed to work. You already know that, Ma."

"You're not allowed to steal either but it didn't stop y'all from doing it."

"Momma, it wasn't me. Hello, I didn't catch a charge."

"It better not had been you." Momma showed tough love. She was the main reason I kept my nose clean.

I knew Ms. Janice Parker didn't play that crap.

"Do you need anything, Jermaine? You know I'm making more money at my new job," she said.

"I don't need any money; I'm good." I meant it too. I had people that made sure I was all right.

"You better promise me you're not lying because no child of mine will ever have to steal. What y'all did was embarrassing."

"I'm sorry but it wasn't me."

"Well, you need to choose your friends more wisely. Next time, think, baby. People are watching every move you make. It comes with the territory. You have people waiting for you to screw up because it makes them mad to see you successful. For every person that loves you, there's one who hates you. One day you're going to listen to me."

"I do listen."

"Sure you do. Bye," she said, hanging up on me.

The next day, we chose to make a public apology. After that, we put everything behind us. As a result, the bad cloud lingering over our heads disappeared. We were free to concentrate on playing ball without most of the negativity.

Two days following our public apology, we made a big statement against #18 Florida St. Eric had stepped into the starting lineup and had a good game. Although we had a minor setback, we balled. Mario responded to the controversy with his game. He had put up huge numbers, giving the media a real reason to talk. I was happy for him because he could've laid down while the media dogged him for making a mistake. In essence, we all could've let it affect us but we remained mentally tough through the adversity.

After we'd defeated Florida St., everybody was ready for Christmas break. I couldn't wait to go back home.

* * *

I headed home for a few days during Christmas break. A break was long overdue. Although I enjoyed living in Gainesville, there was no place like home. Scott had rented me a Cadillac Escalade and I didn't waste a second getting on the road.

The moment I entered Dade County, I called everyone, which I regretted. It became a tug-of-war battle because everybody wanted to hang out with me later on.

While riding through town, I popped up to Coach Baxter's front door. Everyone was happy to see me. I felt like I owed them everything for taking me in.

After saying hello to everyone, Coach and I talked outside alone. He encouraged me to remain tough and focused through the madness. That meant a lot to me coming from him.

After our talk, Lindsey snuck away with me. We were happy to see each other. I couldn't wait to take her home to meet my peoples. At every stoplight, we were tonguing each other down. "Get a room, morons!" someone shouted as we held up traffic.

"Fuck off, asshole!" Lindsey yelled out the window.

I laughed.

Momma's face lit up when she saw me at the front door. She pulled me into the house in a rush. "Look who's here, everybody!"

I grabbed Lindsey's hand. All of my family was at the house on Christmas Eve. Half of them, I didn't know or recognize, but they seemed happy to meet me. My cousins were sitting in the living room staring at Lindsey.

"Everybody this is my friend Lindsey," I said.

The room got quiet for a few seconds.

My uncle broke the silence. "Nice to meet you, Lindsey."

My cousins rolled their eyes and started whispering.

"I know somebody made me a sweet potato pie?" I said.

"Nana made you a few," Momma said.

I pulled Lindsey in the kitchen with me. My folks were sitting at the table while the pots whistled with steam. There were so many pots and pans of food that it seemed like Thanksgiving.

"What's going on, peeps?" I said.

My long-lost uncle gave me a big hug – the one who thought he was better than everybody. He retired from the military and made big bucks as a recruiting manager. "Look at my nephew," Uncle Gary said, looking me over. "I can't believe how big you've grown."

"What, you thought I was gonna stay a li'l pipsqueak?"

He threw up his set and started dancing like Muhammad Ali. "You still aren't too big to get knocked out."

I put up my set too. "Don't make me dust you off, old man."

He backed away and everybody started laughing. After playing around with him, I introduced everyone else to Lindsey.

My grandmother gave her a genuine hug. "How are you, honey?" she said.

Lindsey smiled. "Great."

"You are gorgeous."

Lindsey blushed. "Thank you."

My auntie Debra Ann looked her over closely. "Yeah, she is a doll. Come sit down, girl."

Lindsey sat at the table. My peoples were friendly. Once they broke her in, she talked up a storm.

I cut a slice of sweet potato pie. It was good. I sat down at the table beside Lindsey. "Taste it," I said, putting my fork to her mouth.

She tasted it.

"Good, ain't it?"

"It's delicious."

My uncle folded his arms and looked at me while he stood at the kitchen sink. "What's your game plan, my man?" he said.

"Game plan?"

"Are you going pro next year or what?"

I shrugged.

Roy walked in the kitchen with bags of groceries. I stood up and showed him the proper respect in his house.

"How's it going?" he said.

"Good," I said, patting him on the back.

"So?" Uncle Gary said.

"I really haven't thought about it yet," I lied.

"I think you need to."

Momma walked in the kitchen during the middle of the conversation.

"I'm sure your mama's tired of job hopping," he said.

"Excuse me?" Momma said.

"I was telling Jermaine he needs to consider the pros while the getting is good."

"You need to mind your own goddamn business. He's intelligent enough to make his own decisions, contrary to what you may think."

"I'm only saying, Janice, he's got the opportunity to help the family."

"Oh, now you want to talk about family? Where was the family when he needed clean shoes and clothes on his back? Let's not talk about family. Okay, Gary?"

"I think you must've forgotten who helped you get out of debt one time. Till this day, I still haven't seen one red cent of my money."

My grandmother played peacemaker. "Y'all need to cut out all this mess. The devil is a liar . . ."

I left the kitchen because my peoples were tripping. Lindsey and I sat in the den and watched TV. My peoples had me upset because I came home to relieve stress, not pile on more. We heard them arguing in the kitchen like children. I was tired of everybody trying to decide what I should do with my life. It was a never-ending story.

Half the day slipped away while everyone walked around mad. I couldn't believe it. Uncle Gary walked past me. "Go for the money," he said, stepping out the front door.

"Gary, stop it," Auntie Debra Ann said, following him outside. Then they started arguing over the matter.

Dinnertime was special. Everybody let go of their grudges and had a good time. It started getting late. Lindsey seemed ready to go like me. I wrapped my arms around her shoulders at the dinner table. "I love you," I whispered.

She looked at me as if I were full of it.

"I'm serious; I want you back in my life."

My friends were ringing my cell phone nonstop. Kevin left back-to-back messages. I picked up the phone when I saw Bones' number. He had talked me into going out, although I didn't need to. After I got off the phone, I told everybody goodnight and headed out the door.

I picked up Bones from around the block. Lindsey was upset at me as she sat on the passenger's side. She seemed worried that I was gonna end up in trouble. It drove me crazy that she and my mother thought alike. Bones lit a joint and she gave me the evil eye. I made him put it out before she had a fit.

When I dropped Lindsey off home, she asked me to step out of the truck. "Where are you going?" she said.

"I don't know."

"Why do you do this to me?"

"Do what?"

"Keep me on edge."

"What's with you? You're worried about the wrong things."

"At least I care. That's more than I can say for your friends. Have you ever thought to yourself what if you're stopped with marijuana in the car?"

"Oh my God, if you don't sound like my mother. Please stop, it's driving me crazy, yo."

"Oh gee fucking whiz! I try to help and this is the thanks I get?" She walked away upset.

I grabbed her before she made it to the front door. "Stop taking life so seriously."

"No, maybe you should start taking life seriously." She walked in the house and slammed the door.

I dug deep into my pockets and looked to the starlit sky wishing for a perspective on life. She had me wondering if I should go.

I got in my truck, giving it a second thought.

Bones looked at me. "You good to go?" he said.

"Yeah, bro."

Bones lit his joint and parlayed. He and I strolled by a few parties. They were nothing special. We rode around town for an hour looking for fun. Bones suggested Tootsie's Cabaret. Supposedly it was one of the best gentlemen's clubs in Miami. I was hesitant because I had never been to a strip club and besides I didn't have money to throw away on girls. "I don't know about the strip club. There's gotta be something else we can find to do. I'm not interested in wasting money," I said.

Bones shook his head. "You got it twisted. The strip club is one place you shouldn't mind spendin' yo' dough. I'ont know whatchu been smokin' lately. I think you scared of pussy."

"Scared? Never that, bro."

"Then let's hit it."

I got in using a fake ID. The place was huge with expensive Plasma screens. Neon lights lit up the club like a Las Vegas casino. It was an upscale place filled with tall, short, thick, and thin strippers of all colors. Most of them looked Brazilian.

Bones and I sat watching the action from the main floor. Some of the girls weren't that hot. "We shoulda gone to King of Diamonds," he said.

"Let's go."

Someone gripped my shoulder. When I turned my head, Louie was standing over me. "¿Qué pasa, homie?" he said.

"Chilling."

"You amigos having a great time?"

I grinned. "Most def."

Louie shook his head. "Come with me, amigos."

We followed Louie upstairs to VIP. He had his own private room. VIP was the best. We had a view of the entire club along with plush seating. All the girls were a perfect ten as opposed to the ones on the main floor. I was in awe. A few NFL players were in VIP throwing away cash. They had a caseload of champagne; $150 a bottle was nothing for them to blow while I only had twenty-five dollars in my pocket.

A curvaceous Brazilian stripper approached me. Fully nude, she coiled her body around me. My face lit up like a child on Christmas Day. I gave her all of my money and she left me starving for another lap dance. I was hooked as I reached down into my empty pockets. Louie could see it in my eyes. He handed me a huge stack of twenty-dollar bills bounded by a rubber band.

Throughout the night, Bones and I used every dime. We had spent a fortune in the skybox, a private room with full friction. The lights were dimmed as I watched a cinnamon-complexioned Latina stripper get loose for cash. She was beautiful. At the snap of Louie's fingers, she unzipped my jeans.

"Hold up, chill, mami," I said, pushing her away.

"Stop acting like a homo. Why do you think God gave us such beautiful creatures?" he said. Louie got up and looked at the exotic dancer. "Take good care of him, el bebé."

She smiled and dug into my pants. "Mi placer."

The woman gave me a night to remember. It was a night of fun that had me addicted to strip clubs.

* * *

After a night of fun at the strip joint, I knocked on my mother's door at six in the morning. I'd freshened up at Bones' crib because the smell of sex and alcohol was all over me, and I didn't want my mother tripping.

She opened the door and put a hand on her hip. "Do you know I thought something happened to you?"

I walked in the house and gave her a big hug. "Merry Christmas, Momma."

"Merry Christmas to you too but you don't play fair. Where were you?"

"That's a secret," I said, plopping on the couch. The Christmas tree was lit up and I felt like a child all over again.

Sasha and Tiffany ran into the living room and threw themselves in front of the tree. As they prepared to open their gifts, Momma told them to wait on their father.

They pouted.

Sasha started shaking her present from me. She begged me to tell her what it was but I didn't fold under pressure.

Momma sat down beside me. "Could you believe your Uncle Gary yesterday?"

"Nothing surprises me when people see opportunity in front of their eyes."

"That's true but the nerve of him to try and manipulate you."

"Can't nobody make me do anything I don't wanna do. That's one decision I'm gonna make when I'm ready. Sometimes I do think about it. You work too hard."

"I told you, Jermaine, the best thing you can do for me and for yourself is to get a good education."

"I am."

"That way you'll have something to fall back on in case you want to do other things in life."

Roy walked into the living room and wished everyone a Merry Christmas. I wished him a Merry Christmas too. Everyone started opening their gifts. The smile on my mother's face was priceless when I gave her a $100 gift card to Macy's. "Who's bright idea was this?" she said.

"Lindsey's."

"Go figure. Tell her I said thank you – and thank you too."

I knew Momma liked nice things, but her priority was always making sure that we had everything we needed. Every blue moon, she used to buy herself a pretty dress. It made me happy to see her smile.

Roy gave her a housecoat and a pair of cheap-looking earrings. He always came half stepping. Prime example, he always drove the best car to work while she was stuck driving an old beat-up Saturn. I thought my mother deserved much better.

Momma handed me a gift from her, Roy, and the girls. It was a bottle of Sean John cologne and a polo shirt. "We hope you like it," she said.

"Thanks but y'all didn't have to go all out for me," I said.

"I picked out the shirt," Sasha said.

"You got good taste. The girlies gonna be all over me now," I said, sniffing the cologne. Sasha and Tiffany giggled.

"Hopefully, the shirt fits," Momma said.

"How much was everything?"

"Don't worry about it. You're worth every dime," she said.

I enjoyed a beautiful Christmas with my family like old times sake.

That same day, I got a couple hours of rest and then headed back to Gainesville. We had a game in a couple of days and I couldn't get caught lagging behind.

Scott called me while I was on the highway pushing it at 100 mph. "Merry Christmas!" he said.

"Thanks, man, same to you."

"How's your family?"

"Everyone's doing okay."

"That's great to hear. Let me know if you need anything, Jermaine. I'm here for you."

"Sure thing, Scott."

Scott always looked out for me. He made sure that Momma and I was financially all right. Although I knew he was willing and able to do anything for us, I never milked the cow.

After I hung up with Scott, Kevin called me. I didn't feel up to talking to him. Lately he had a strange way of making me feel bad because things weren't going his way. When I didn't pick up, he left a message.

"I see what time it is now. You sheisty!" he said and hung up.

I sensed the anger in his tone and called him back. "What's up, bro?"

"It's like that, huh? That's how we do it now? Ignore each other's phone calls?"

"Come on, bro. I got a little tied up."

"Where are you?"

"On my way back to school."

"That's creep. I thought we were gonna hang out?"

"I barely had enough time to spend with my own family."

"Is that so? I heard you were all in the booty club. Keep it real."

"I'm gonna always keep it real."

"You haven't kept it real since you've been up the road, man." Kevin got under my skin.

I didn't understand where all the anger was coming from when I thought we were cool. "Look, you got a problem but it ain't with me; it's with yourself. You can't keep blaming everybody, bro," I said.

Finally, he came to his senses. "I'm sorry. I just wanted to kick it like old times, you know?" He started crying.

I wanted to tell him to man up but I couldn't fix my lips to say it. "Man, it's gonna be okay."

After we hung up, I took a deep breath. It seemed like my success brought a lot of people pain.

* * *

When I woke up the next morning, I heard Trey Songz singing "Can't Be Friends." And the room smelled like rich vanilla. Kim walked across the room in an orange turtleneck sweater and a pair of designer jeans. She sat down on the bed and put on a pair of high heel boots.

My phone rang. "What up, Ricky?" I said.

"You coming out to the hospital today?"

"Yeah, bro. Give me an hour," I said.

Whenever Ricky had the chance, he would spend time visiting ill children at the hospital. He was special because many of us were too busy. Somehow, he found the time and energy to give back. Ricky had been begging me to come with him because one of the kids was eager to meet me. "Don't let me down. I told Tommy you were coming, so call me when you're ready," he said.

"Alright peace," I said, hanging up. Then I got out of bed and said, "Good morning."

Kim smiled. "Hey, baby." She grabbed her Coach bag and handed me a set of keys to her car and apartment.

"What'd you want me to do with 'em?"

"Those are your set of keys. You never go home anyway."

I winked. "Oh okay, that's what's up. What's next, the key to your heart?"

"You already have it and you better not abuse it."

Ricky came and picked me up. We spent half the morning at Shands Hospital visiting cancer patients. It was my first time stepping foot inside the hospital. It made me feel good to bring smiles to so many faces. One boy named Tommy had a poster of me and a replica of my jersey in his room. His pale face looked extremely sickly. It almost brought tears to my eyes when I was told he only had six months to live. I took a picture with him and it made his day. It also made my day to know that I had a positive effect on his life.

I walked out of the hospital counting my blessings.

18

THE NEW YEAR KICKED OFF good. Despite the shoplifting controversy, I appeared on the cover of *Sports Illustrated*. Inside the cover gave the world a glance at my work ethic and dedication to the game of basketball. I shared a lot of personal information too. I let it be known that my mother was the reason I stayed on the right path. When she read the article, she cried like a baby.

After *Sports Illustrated* revealed me to the world, there came more pressure. I was expected to be superman although I was only human.

Throughout the month, I held up to everyone's expectations on the basketball court. I was at the top of my game averaging 19.5 points, 6 assists, 8 rebounds, and 2.5 steals. My team balled as we faced tough competition in our conference. We knocked off #12 Georgia, # 20 South Carolina, #13 Tennessee, #8 Arkansas, then we headed out west and defeated #10 Auburn. The tougher the competition, the harder we brought it.

In a close game against #5 Kentucky, I sunk the winning shot, making ESPN's top play of the week. Our squad was resilient. I could foresee a national championship this year. March Madness was on my mind as opposed to the NBA draft like everyone had expected. In the wake of my success, sports analysts projected me as a potential number-one draft pick.

Saturday evening, we arrived back in town from Kentucky. It was a bumpy flight. I didn't think we were gonna make it. When we touched ground, I took a deep breath. Gator Fans greeted us as we walked through the airport victoriously. Scott wouldn't let me enjoy the moment as he tried to convince me over the phone to declare for the NBA draft.

When I got back to the dorms, I had a package from him. He had sent me a couple of tickets to the Lakers-Heat game next month. I laid across bed looking at other mail addressed to me. People sent me all kinds of things from souvenirs to lingerie. I trashed a pair of stinky panties that a beautiful blond had sent to me.

Devin looked at the girl's half-naked photos and got the panties out of the garbage can. "How could you not love that smell?" he said, sniffing them.

"Man, that's nasty." I got tired of going through piles of junk and tossed it aside.

I began contemplating the draft. Scott had me rethinking my future considering the type of season I was having. A few questions came to mind while facing the decision of leaving school early, like could I match the overall success of this year if I stayed, and could I remain injury free in the process?

When I thought about the core components of our team leaving, it enticed me to make a move too. Mario and Ricky had announced their decisions. It was hard to visualize making a run at a national championship without them but I knew anything was possible with the rising talent on our team. Scott had me seriously stuck in limbo.

* * *

One evening, Scott showed up in town. He and I ate dinner at Mark's Prime Steakhouse. I cut through a tender piece of steak while I listened to him press me about the draft.

"You have a shot at being a number-one pick," he kept emphasizing. "There's nothing else here for you to prove."

"I wanna get my degree."

He clapped and everyone in the restaurant looked at us. "That's excellent!" he said. "I commend you but this opportunity may never come knocking at your door again. It's not often that a first-year player gets a shot at being a number-one pick."

I moved my plate to the side and made room for dessert. The waitress set a plate of key lime pie in front of me. She was a cutie.

Scott snapped his fingers as I watched her walk away. "Hey, snap out of it," he said.

"How can you be so sure that I'll get drafted in the first round?"

He looked at me as if I were a fool for thinking otherwise.

"Alright never mind, forget I asked," I said. As I sat and ate my pie, he made the money sound good. I couldn't imagine sitting on an eight million dollar contract.

"So what's it going to be?" he said.

Even though the money was enticing, I couldn't miss what I never had. "I need a little bit more time."

Scott sighed. "Okay, take all the time you need, but remember, this opportunity may never come again."

Ten minutes later, the waitress came back to the table with the tab. Scott placed $100 on the table. "You really need to think long and hard about this."

I saluted him. "Yes, sir."

When I got back to the dorms that night, I thought on it until I ended up dozing off.

* * *

The month of February was tough for our basketball team. We were sliding downhill, losing two back-to-back conference games. Coach sat me down with three minutes left in regulation against Kentucky. I had played my heart out even though I had a season-low 8 points on 3-for-14 shooting.

We were getting embarrassed on our own home court, down sixteen points. I grabbed a towel and wiped the sweat off my face. Then I covered my head because I refused to watch the rest of the game. I was down on myself for turning the ball over six times.

After the game, Yakhouba and I sat at the press conference alongside Coach. Coach took the brunt of the questions although we were bombarded with questions too.

"Jermaine, can you state the reason this team was unable to match the energy of Kentucky this time around?"

"I think they wanted it more."

A reporter directed his question to Coach. "Unforced turnovers were key in this game. How do you get your team to establish that sense of trust and camaraderie it had at the beginning of the season?"

"We have an amazing group of guys . . . they'll figure it out."

After the press conference, I trudged out of the building. I knew that game was on me.

I watched ESPN's highlights of the game for most of the night. Then I went to bed.

Kim eased to my side of the bed and touched me like she wanted some action.

"Please don't touch me," I said, turning away.

"What's wrong with you?"

"I'm not in the mood right now."

"Well excuse me," she said, snatching the covers off me.

Half the night, I stared into the dark. Having a bad game was like torture. I couldn't sleep for nothing in the world. When I looked at the clock, it was 1:30 a.m. I started rubbing on Kim's thigh until I was aroused. "You awake?"

"I'm not in the mood right now."

I got up and started putting on my clothes.

She sat up and looked at me. "Where are you going?"

I sat on the bed and slid on my shoes. "You must don't know who I am, girl."

Kim hopped up quickly. Then she got down on her knees in front of me. "Please, don't go," she begged. "I'll do anything for you."

"Will you move out my way?"

"No," she said, burying her head in my lap.

"You gotta give me a reason to stay." After I decided to stay, she gave me the green light.

When I finished smashing, Kim grabbed me and whispered, "I love you."

* * *

The next morning, I got up for class and left her keys on the counter. After class, Mario and I headed to practice. Practice was brutal. Coach was angry over last night's loss. He worked us extra hard. The excessive workload put a strain on our bodies. I was aching with back spasms and sat out the rest of practice.

Two days later, we won our next game against #18 Vanderbilt. We had won seven of nine conference games, peaking to #2 in the polls. At a record of 25-3, we had six games left in the season. On several occasions this year, my name was mentioned as a candidate for multiple awards like SEC Player of the Year, AP Player of the Year, and the list went on. The AP Player of the Year Award was the most impressive to me, considering only three others in my class had received the honor. At times, I tried not to think about it because I didn't wanna jinx myself.

After the game that night, I lay across bed with a heating pad on my back. Lindsey and I were on the phone for a couple of hours. Finally, we agreed to get back together. I was a happy man. While I was on the phone, Kim showed up to the dorms unexpectedly.

I put Lindsey on hold and stepped outside the door. "Can I help you?"

"Why haven't you returned my messages?" she said.

"I've been busy, and don't be popping up at my door."

"All of a sudden you're busy, huh? Did I do something wrong?"

"No."

"Then why did you leave my keys on the counter?"

"Look, it's late. I gotta go."

"You aren't even man enough to tell me."

"Humph, I'm all man. You already know that, baby," I said, grabbing my package.

She shook her head. "You make me sick! I knew I shouldn't have trusted your black ass."

"Are you finished?"

The girl snapped and started swinging at me. I felt her nails dig into my face. We were in the middle of the hall fighting like cats and dogs. Before I knew it, campus security was at my door. Somebody had called the police too. The police didn't give me a chance to tell my side of the story. They immediately escorted me out of the building in cuffs. A small crowd of people was gathered around the yard, watching the drama take place

I was embarrassed as I stood outside in my drawers, explaining what'd happened. The cops didn't wanna hear what I had to say although I was the one bleeding. "Look at my face, Officer," I said, pleading my case.

An Asian kid, who watched the whole thing, came to my defense. I thanked God because the police were ready to haul me off to jail.

It was a close call.

* * *

The next evening, I snuck in town for the Heat-Lakers game. I picked up Bones and we had a good time. It was a packed house at the American Airlines Arena. D-Wade was on fire. I enjoyed watching him play. He shook Kobe and stopped on a dime, nailing a pull-up jumper in the lane.

I looked at Bones and shook my head. "The boy is sick," I said, sipping the alcohol in my Styrofoam cup.

Bones, a die-hard Lakers' fan, couldn't stand it. "It ain't over yet!" he yelled at the Laker hater in the row behind us.

Kobe ran back down the court and hit a three-pointer.

The crowd groaned.

Bones got a kick out of teasing Heat fans. "Kobe is the man! Wade don't want no static with the Black Mamba!"

I sat back and analyzed the game. The Heat had too much firepower for the Lakers. Fourth quarter, the game had gotten away from L.A. With four minutes left in regulation, we eased our way out of the arena. I had to be back to Gainesville the same night.

Bones and I got inside of my rental truck and made it out of the parking lot while traffic was easy. Bones poured me a cup of liquor. I took a few sips as I sped through downtown Miami toward signs leading to Interstate 95. Bones took out the cigarette lighter and lit a joint. He puffed and passed.

"Nah, I'm good, bro," I said.

I took a sip from my cup. My phone rang, falling to the floor as I reached inside my pocket to get it. All game long, it had been ringing nonstop. I swerved as I reached to the floor. When I looked up, police lights were flashing in my rear view. "Damn put that crap out!" I said.

"Oh shit," Bones said, scrambling. He stuffed a bag of marijuana under the seat and tossed the bottle of alcohol in the back.

I was nervous as I pulled over to the left shoulder of the street. A brother walked over to the truck cautiously. I thanked God.

"Both of you gentleman put your hands where I can see them," he said.

We obeyed his orders.

"How are you doing tonight, Officer?" I said pleasantly.

"I'm great. Do you realize that you almost ran over the curb? Have you been drinking?"

"I was reaching for my phone and made a mistake and swerved."

"That's not what I asked you."

"Yes, I had a few drinks at the arena."

"It smells like you boys have been smoking reefer too."

Bones leaned forward in his seat. "Officer, it was me."

"Did I ask you anything?"

Bones sat back and shut his mouth. The officer looked at me as if he recognized my face. "Let me see your license and registration. Is your license good, Parker?" he said, shining his flashlight on me.

"Yes, sir."

"If everything comes back clean I'll let you go."

I searched for my license and the registration to the rental truck. The officer started talking basketball. "You boys forgot to show up against Kentucky, huh?"

"You got jokes," I said.

A long-necked, pale-faced officer pulled up on a motorcycle to assist him. He walked over and stood on post. "Everything's alright?" he said.

"Yes, I have it under control."

The officer sniffed the air. "Hootie hoo, I smell weed. This could get exciting."

Damn, I thought.

The pale-faced officer walked to the other side of the truck and made Bones get out. Then he frisked him.

Finally, I handed my license and registration to the brother. He shook his head. "Get out of the truck. What were you thinking?" he whispered. He proceeded with normal procedures and frisked me.

For several minutes, the pale-faced officer searched the truck as if he was determined to find drugs. "Bingo!" he said, holding up a Ziploc bag of marijuana. Then he went back in the truck searching for more paraphernalia.

"Why do y'all do this to yourselves? Man, you have to use your head," the brother said to me. His backup made me take a Breathalyzer test upon finding an open container of alcohol on the driver's side.

Unfortunately, I was over the legal drinking limit. Bones and I were placed in handcuffs while being read our rights.

Karma was a bitch.

1 9

I was disciplined and faced a one-game suspension. I was charged with underage drinking and DUI. The court forced me to pay a $100 fine, and ordered me to take a mandatory alcohol awareness class. Coach spoke to the media on my behalf. I felt awful and it was hard to sleep for the past two weeks. Once again, the media had taken advantage of the opportunity to drag my name through the dirt. I didn't blame any one but myself for the stupidity. I was very hard on myself and nothing hurt me more than not being able to play basketball.

Tuesday night's game against #15 Louisiana State, I didn't travel with the team. Coach thought it was best in order to avoid distraction to the team. I stayed in the dorms and watched us struggle on offense. Mario was on his game but the rest of the team couldn't get it going. The offense looked totally out of synch.

I turned off the TV because I couldn't stand to watch my team struggle. After lying in bed depressed, I picked up the phone and called Lindsey. She was the only one who understood me, while my mother was judgmental towards me, like the columnists who wrote hurtful things about me.

Lindsey heard me out without throwing crap in my face. "Let it be a lesson learned and move on," she said.

"Do you think I'm a bad person?"

"No, but you're stubborn."

"I don't know why I'm this way."

"Stop being so hard on yourself, okay? You're human."

"Tell that to all those people who expect me to be a role model."

"That's their problem if they don't want to take responsibility. Everyone is always looking for someone to blame."

"You're right. Let me stop tripping and get on with my life."

"I mean like really."

I was determined to get through the adversity and help lead my team to a national championship.

* * *

At the beginning of March, my list of troubles began to grow. I was under investigation by the NCAA. The fancy rental cars, game tickets, and connection to Scott brought on suspicion. There was speculation that I received money and gifts from Scott who was a certified agent. When I learned of this, I was worried out of my mind.

During the ongoing investigation, I sat down with the board of athletic directors. It was determined that I was suspended for the rest of the season. The decision hit me hard. I felt like everything had been taken away from me. For days, I bawled like a baby, as my future seemed uncertain. Every day it was hard to function with the drama surrounding my circumstances. I was the talk of the town and the media's punching bag. I had shut everyone out while I sorted things out. I had a lot of important decisions to make concerning my future.

One week when Momma couldn't get in touch with me, she sent a messenger. "Ey, Jermaine, your moms said call her ASAP," Devin said, tossing me the portable phone, as I walked out of the bathroom.

Finally, I let down my guard and talked to her. Momma was calm and understanding. She encouraged me to stay focused in school. I took a deep breath out of frustration because I didn't wanna hear it.

"Hello, are you listening to me?" she said.

"Yes."

"One thing about it: basketball is a privilege but education is your right. Take advantage of it . . ."

I let her do all the talking because she always had to be right. Although she made perfect sense, I wasn't ready to hang up my dreams.

A week later, I received a call from Scott while watching TV in bed. All week the media speculated that I would declare for the draft. I remained quiet while the rumors spread. Scott was taken by the news too. He advised me to declare for the NBA draft despite missing significant games. Even though I had missed the last six games of the season, I had made a mark. I received votes to the All-SEC First Team, but all other awards were snubbed due to violation of NCAA rules. Despite that, Scott believed I would be selected in the top 5 of the draft, if I sought eligibility.

After we hung up, I thought about it. Then I thought of all I would be leaving behind, like a chance to redeem my name and a shot at a championship. I was kicking myself for letting everyone down. The most disappointing thing was watching my team make a run at the national championship without being a part of it. Through it all, Coach supported me a hundred percent and encouraged me to come back strong next season.

I figured my life could be worse when Devin stormed in the room pissed off about his STD test results. He'd tested positive for herpes and assumed he'd contracted the disease from Marie.

I was shocked because she looked clean. "You sure?" I said.

"I'm positive she gave it to me. She's the only one I've been bangin' without a condom."

"Wow."

"You can't trust none of these damn hoes." He plopped on the bed and started cursing the ground Marie walked on.

I started scratching my head.

The next day, I went to a clinic to get tested. I drove to a location where I couldn't be easily spotted. It was early, too, so I could be the first one in and the first one out. I was praying the whole time as I sat in the office with one other boy. I began to count all the women I had smashed without protection. There were two, but I vowed to wrap it up after this crap.

When my name was called, I broke out in a sweat. I gave blood, praying my results came back negative.

After two days, I received my results. I was lucky. I tested negative for an STD. That was one thing off my back.

I walked across campus feeling relieved. My headphones were on blast as I sung "Whatever You Like" by T.I. I put a dollar in the vending machine for some Skittles. Suddenly, the pesky agent named Dwight, popped up from behind the machine. I almost dropped my iPod. "Man, are you serious?" I said, catching it.

"Didn't mean to catch you off guard. Do you have a minute to spare?"

"No," I said, walking away.

He trailed me as he pitched his agency. The brother was stubborn and persistent. "I could make big things happen for your career . . ."

I put back on my headphones because he wouldn't take no for an answer.

"Please take my card. You should really give me the opportunity to guide your career, Jermaine Parker. I'm telling you, we'll make a great team," he said.

I took his card and put it in my pocket "Okay, let me think about it."

He shook my hand. "Please do, brother. We have to stick together, you understand me?"

"Alright." I turned up my music and headed to the weight room.

* * *

After I finished working out, I chilled with my homies. They had a big game around the corner. The NCAA tournament kicked off in Atlanta next week. I knew it was gonna be hard to watch from the bench. The thought of it brought me down.

Tyreke and I sat at the edge of the couch, getting high inside of Ricky's apartment. My homie took a few puffs and then passed it back to me.

Ricky shook his head. "Y'all need to stop poisoning your bodies. Your body is the temple of God."

I laughed. "You act like everything is a sin."

"How is herb poison? It's a natural substance grown from the earth. God put it here for a reason," Tyreke said.

I gave Tyreke high five. "Y'all ever heard of Dwight Black?" I said.

"Make sure you run in the opposite direction. He's a straight crook," Ricky said.

"For real?"

"If you don't want to take my word for it ask around. He gives a lot of black agents a bad rep."

Mario walked in the door with his fiancée. Ciara frowned when she smelled weed.

"Hey, y'all need to take that somewhere else," he snapped. Anytime his girl was around, his whole demeanor changed. He worshipped the ground she walked on. By all means, I couldn't blame him. Ciara was a beautiful sister who deserved much respect. She carried herself like a lady, unlike a lot of the girls who acted like tramps.

Tyreke and I grabbed our things and left.

When I got back to the dorms, I stretched out and watched the tournament predictions on ESPN. My cell phone kept ringing in the middle of the night. The girls were worse than us when their hormones started raging. I turned off my phone because I wasn't in the mood. I had a lot on my mind and girls weren't one of them. The dollar signs were calling my name. Scott had me excited at the idea of being picked in the top 5. I had a lot on my plate right now.

20

AFTER OUR WIN IN THE first round against #15 Jackson St., I ran out on the court and hugged Ricky. He carried the team on his shoulders.

"That's how you do that shit!" I said, knuckling him in the chest. Then I stepped back and let him and Mario do their interview from courtside. Somehow, the camera found its way in my face. I shunned the media, giving them my butt to kiss.

Two days later, we faced #10 Maryland in the second round. I sat the bench and watched a ten-point lead evaporate in the second half. We had gone cold. Neither Ricky nor Mario could buy a bucket. I shook my head when Ricky fouled his man on a three-point attempt.

Time was our worst enemy.

A three-point deficit grew larger with four minutes left in regulation. Coach had called a timeout to regroup. I tried to motivate my teammates but they weren't in the mood for a pep talk. Their confidence seemed shaken. They went back on the court and played hard to the last minute though. Unfortunately, we were unable to respond to a miraculous 18-2 run.

The Terps began to celebrate and their fans got louder as time trickled down. It was heartbreaking because it was the end of something special. Everyone was trying to hold back their tears, including me. I knew my time had run out and I had a big decision to make.

21

I ANNOUNCED MY DECISION TO enter the NBA draft. My mother supported my decision even though she had encouraged me to stay in school. It was a hard decision to leave school. I had formed a bond with Coach and my teammates that was special. It was as if I had abandoned my family. I was definitely a Gator for life. Orange and blue ran through my veins.

I stayed put in Gainesville until the NBA Combine in Orlando, Fl. Every day, I worked on strengthening and conditioning. I worked on my game too; I played in pickup games with several other NBA prospects. I wanted it bad. Everything was riding on me getting selected in the draft, like the expensive gifts and money I received from Scott. I had given Momma money to pay property taxes and to pay off other debt; and he had furnished me with my own apartment. My list of obligations to my agent was growing by the day.

One afternoon, Scott showed up to my apartment in a spotless all-black Mercedes Benz. We talked business over lunch at Sawamura's Japanese Steak House. He enlightened me on a list of teams that were interested in me. Toronto, New Jersey, Detroit, Milwaukee, and Miami had me on their radar. I was willing to go to any team that would take me, although playing for Miami would've been icing on the cake.

After lunch, we headed outside. Scott surprised me with a big gift. He handed me a set of keys to the 600 Benz. "I thought it would be a great gift for all your troubles," he said, tapping me on the shoulder.

My mouth dropped. "I don't believe you, Scott!"

He smiled. "What can I say? You're worth it." A taxi rolled up at the curb and Scott opened the door.

"The least I can do is drive you to the airport," I said.

"This is one time I'm going to have to tell you no." Scott got in the taxi and waved goodbye.

"You're the man, Scott!"

As the taxi rolled off, he hung out the window and shouted, "No, you're the man!"

I anxiously started bouncing on my toes as I tried to open the door. I mistakenly set off the alarm. A valet parker came over and helped me.

"Thanks, bro," I said.

"No problem, dude," he smiled.

When I got in on the driver's side, I felt like a million bucks.

* * *

That night, I headed to the club with Mario and Tyreke. Most of the girls flocked to us like flies on crap. We took advantage of our status and partied like rock stars. Tyreke had met a gorgeous half-breed sister in the club. She had to be one of the finest women in the club. Mario and I watched Tyreke grind up against her body as we chilled.

I walked out of the club wasted. My homies hopped in the car and we headed back to my place. Tyreke was in the back seat with the gorgeous sister he'd met in the club. I looked at them through my rearview. Tyreke's head was nudged between her breasts. All of a sudden, Mario and I smelled a strong odor. We turned around and he was fingering the girl.

I got mad. "Tyreke, chill!" I said, cracking the windows.

Mario started cracking up. "That's a funny character."

My cell phone rang. Lindsey surprised me with good news that she would be here in a couple of days. I was excited about seeing my girl. After all, it didn't make sense to have the world and no one to share it with.

As soon as I got home, I cleaned the back seat and sprayed it down with cologne. When I walked back in my apartment, Mario was standing in the doorway of my bedroom, smiling.

"What are you fools up to, man?" I said. I looked in my room. Tyreke had his pants to the floor receiving a heavy-duty blowjob.

"She's a beast," Mario said, laughing.

The girl smiled at us as she did her thing. I walked away because I didn't want anything to do with it. In the meantime, I laid on the couch and watched *Silent Library*. Thirty minutes later, I got up to check on those cats. Mario and Tyreke were like a tag team. One was at the head and the other at the tail. Mario held his cell phone, taping himself receiving a blowjob.

Tyreke called me as he nailed it from behind. "You want some of this ham?" he said, laughing

"Nah, I'm cool, bro." I watched them switch positions and double penetrate the girl like a hardcore porno flick. She let them do all kinds of things to her body without a complaint.

"Jermaine, bring your ass over here, dawg," Mario said.

"I'm good."

After all the action, Mario and Tyreke had fun ejaculating on the girl. She seemed to enjoy it.

* * *

Two days later, the police showed up to my door. It was early in the morning. I looked over my shoulder as Lindsey stood in the kitchen fixing breakfast. "What's the problem, Officer?" I said.

"We need to take you in for questioning."

"For what?" I stepped halfway outside the door.

"We have a young lady who claims she was sexually assaulted at this apartment."

"You can't be serious?"

"We have two individuals in custody and we ask for your cooperation in this matter." They handcuffed me and read me my rights.

"Look, I didn't touch that woman! She's lying," I said.

Lindsey ran out of the kitchen and asked me what was going on.

"I have no idea," I said.

"Jermaine, don't frigging lie to me. What did you do?"

"I told you, nothing!"

The officers sat me down on the couch and began asking questions. One of the officers walked through my apartment while the other officer tended to me. Lindsey picked up on the conversation quickly.

"No one made her do anything against her will. The sex was consensual, Officer. The last thing I would ever do is rape a female."

Lindsey looked at me as if I were a criminal when in actuality I was the victim. "I can't believe you would do this to me!" She slapped me and screamed, "I hate your fucking guts!"

"Miss, calm down! If you strike him again you're going to jail," the officer warned.

"I didn't do anything," I said.

"Just shut up; I don't want to hear it," she said.

I hopped up angrily. "Damn it, you know I would never do anything that stupid! What the hell is wrong with you?"

The officer seemed scared. "I don't want to hear another outburst from you!" he said, grabbing his gun.

I shook my head and sat back down. The thought of serving jail time for a crime I didn't commit scared me to death.

Lindsey stared at me with tears in her eyes. They began to fall when the police walked me out the door.

"I swear I'm innocent. Trust me," I begged.

22

I GAVE A TWO-HOUR STATEMENT to a slick-haired detective. During those two hours, I was scared. I thought I was going down because it was obvious he wanted to see me locked up. I told him every single detail that occurred. He had me shaking because it was his word against mine.

Close to an hour later, a bald dark-skinned detective walked into the room looking awfully disappointed. "We have to let him go," he said.

The slick-haired detective slammed his fist down on the table. "Are you fucking kidding me?"

"Go check out the flick in evidence," he said.

"Yes, check it out," I said, relieved.

"Shut your face! I don't want to hear a word out of you, scum-bag," the slick-haired detective said.

"Yes, sir." I cooperated with the detectives to the fullest. The last thing I needed was negative press. They made me stand up, then one of them un-cuffed me.

I thanked God as I walked out of the investigation room a free man. My wrists were sore and bruised from the handcuffs.

Lindsey was in the lobby waiting for me. The sad look on her face was noticeable from afar. When I got closer, her face appeared red and puffy as if she had been crying. "Are you okay?" I said.

She grabbed her things and walked away.

Even though my name was cleared, I still had to face the music. There was a news truck parked in front of the police station. Lindsey handed me the keys to my car. I darted across the parking lot and hopped in the car, avoiding the cameras.

"Jermaine, can you tell us why you were detained?" one reporter shouted.

Lindsey got in on the passenger's side and slammed the door. Then I sped away, leaving the media clueless. Lindsey wouldn't speak two words to me as we headed home.

I broke the silence and said, "Did my mom call?"

"Yes."

"You didn't mention this to her, did you?"

"No."

"I'm sorry for putting you through this crap. You don't deserve it."

"It's like I don't even know who you are anymore."

"I've made a lot of mistakes, but a criminal I am not."

Lindsey wiped the tears from her eyes. "Tell me what happened that night, and you better not lie to me," she sniffled.

I told her every single detail.

"I find it odd that you would allow yourself to be put in that predicament in the first place. You and all your friends are disgusting. I think I'm going to puke."

"I'm sorry that everyone can't be as perfect as you."

"That's irrelevant. The fact of the matter is that you're losing control and you don't even see it."

23

I ARRIVED IN ORLANDO FOR the NBA Combine. A long week of drills, testing, and interviews had turned out to be a breeze. Scott didn't want me to participate at the combine but I'd opted to. He thought it was a risk but I was confident in my ability to rise to the occasion. I had no butterflies. During workouts, I performed well in the strength and agility drills. I showed NBA teams that I was one of the best, if not the best, at the combine. My vertical leap was off the charts and I had the second best sprint time. My physical was on point too; I measured 6-4 ¾ and weighed in at 205 pounds. The NBA scouts and GMs were content with the measurements and physical condition of my body.

One of the top prospects in the draft, Brandon Williams, had become my new best friend as we shared the same stories and fears. He and I were projected to go in the first round according to sources. Brandon prayed that he didn't end up in Toronto while I was excited to go to any team that would pick me. The New Jersey Nets, Los Angeles Clippers, and Detroit Pistons seemed most interested in me when I had spoken with their personnel. I was truly blessed while a lot of my peers could only dream of walking in my shoes. Every night I'd get down on my knees and thank God.

On the third day in Orlando, Brandon and I hit the town. We were treated like royalty as club owners vouched for us to make an appearance at their venues. It seemed as though the town was reserved for us as we rolled to one club in a stretch limo Hummer. Everything was paid in full.

As we made way into the club wearing expensive jewelry, we were surrounded by security. The DJ had "Hotel Room" by Pitbull on blast. Everybody was getting loose. The women in the club were banging. One flashed me with her boobs from across the dance floor.

"Oh wow!" I said, turning my head away. I couldn't believe it.

Brandon laughed. "You better get used to it."

"I need a drink, bro." After a couple of drinks, I loosened up. The temptation of alcohol and women was too hard to resist. I had walked out of the club with a cutie and never returned, as we got acquainted in the back of the limo.

*　*　*

The next morning, it was back to business. I took on questions from the media. My checkered past never came up. Every question pertained to the skills I possessed on the court. I let it be known that I was confident while a lot of people doubted me.

When I got back to the hotel room, my squeeze was in the shower. I felt awful because I couldn't recall her name. I took a peep inside of her handbag and looked at her license, which read Angelina Gutierrez. A couple of seconds later, she turned off the water. Then she walked into the bedroom half-dressed. I was in awe at her beautiful smile and olive-toned skin.

"You're leaving?" I said.

"Yes."

"No, don't leave," I begged.

"I have no clothes and I'm starving."

I handed her a T-shirt out of my suitcase. "Put this on."

"Thank you," she said, sliding on the T-shirt.

I picked up the phone and ordered room service. Thirty minutes later, room service showed up to the door with the best food I'd ever tasted in my life.

Scott called while I feasted on a plate of sirloin tips and vegetables. "Jermaine, how's it going?" he said, sounding excited.

"So far so good. Any good news?"

"Depends on what you're looking to hear."

"Come on, Scott, give it to me raw."

"You may be headed to Los Angeles. The Clippers is a great organization that you know is in the process of rebuilding . . . I don't see them bypassing you if they win the lottery. If they choose to address their weakness at the center position instead of going with the best overall point guard in the draft, then New Jersey could be a potential suitor . . ."

I got up and took a walk out to the balcony. I was thinking California is lovely, but too far away. The idea of playing ball out west didn't excite me. I prayed that I ended up on the east coast. Suddenly, location had me in terrible suspense. "What's the likelihood I'll end up in L.A.?" I said.

"We'll have a clearer picture once you work out for both teams this summer. But once the draft lottery gets underway, it'll definitely give us some sense of where we're headed. Until then your guess is as good as mine."

"Sounds good, Scott." After we hung up, I looked across the balcony wondering what the future held in store for me.

* * *

On the fifth day in Orlando, I interviewed with the GM of the New Jersey Nets. The personnel of the organization drooled over me. Questions regarding my character became a topic of discussion. I was asked about the two separate incidents in Miami that landed me in the slammer.

"Both incidents were bad judgment calls, but I've learned from my mistakes, and I can assure this organization that I am a changed person," I said.

"That's great to hear. What do you think you can bring to this organization?"

"I'm a team player and I have a very strong work ethic. I feel those are the things needed to help build a winning franchise."

The GM nodded his head. "You have to love this kid," he said, leaning back in his chair. Then he smiled at me as if I were a jewel. I had them sold on me.

I called Momma on my way back to the hotel. "What are you doing, Momma?"

"Shopping."

"Did Scott call and tell you the news?"

"No."

"It looks like I may be headed to New Jersey."

"Yay! I am so proud of you but I'll be glad when it's over. I'm tired of people stalking me everywhere I go. I was at the grocery store and a gentleman named Dwight followed me around the whole time. It's ridiculous. He offered to buy my groceries and take me to dinner . . ."

As I sat at the stoplight listening to Momma, a car of fine girls pulled up beside me, waving. It seemed like my car was a magnet for women. "You should've told him to kick rocks. You didn't let him buy you anything, did you?" I said, waving back at the girls.

"Think I didn't?"

"Momma, you have to learn to say no. I already told you about these people and their schemes."

"I'm working on it. When are you coming home?"

I took off on green, leaving those gold-digging females in the dust. "I'm not sure."

"Be safe and I love you." The happiness in Momma's voice had spoken volumes. My mother's happiness meant the world to me.

"Love you too," I said, hanging up.

Seconds later, Lindsey called me.

"What's going on, baby cakes?" I said.

"How are things coming along?"

"We may be headed to New Jersey. The Nets are serious about drafting me."

"Really?"

"That's what I'm hoping. Will you come with me?"

"If we're married, yes."

"Huh? Where are you coming from with this mess?"

"I'm not living with you unless we're married."

"I'm not ready for that. Besides what difference does it make if we're married or not? Either way, I'm gonna take care of you."

"Why not get married?"

"I love you to death but you know I'm not trying to go there right now."

"Well, Jermaine, I refuse to move with you. It's wrong."

"We've been crushing since high school and that's wrong too. Hello."

"It doesn't matter. Besides, my father would never approve of me living with a guy when there's no commitment –"

"I have to go," I said, hanging up. Lindsey had another think coming if she thought I was falling for that trap.

When I got to the hotel, I walked in the room and slammed the door. Angelina paused, as she stood in front of the mirror in a pretty dress and high heels.

"I'm sorry. I didn't mean to scare you," I said.

"Is everything okay?"

"Yes."

Angelina wrapped her arms around my shoulders. She smelled like a bouquet of fresh roses. "Are you sure, pappy?"

"It's personal."

"Let me guess, your girlfriend is a bitch?"

"Wrong." I moved her out of the way and began packing my things to leave.

Angelina sat on the bed. "So you're going to keep me in the dark?"

"Look, I don't even know you. Why don't you leave?"

"Why don't you make me?"

I walked over to the bed and pulled her to her feet. "Don't play with me."

"Get your hands off me," she said, pushing me away.

I pushed her on the bed and got on top. We smiled at each other and got things popping.

After we humped, I got up and watched the sunset. Within an hour, the golden part of the day had turned into a moon-lit sky. I looked over the city and shouted, "Top of the world, baby!"

24

Two weeks later, I arrived in Miami after a successful workout with the Clippers and Nets. While back home, in Miami, I laid low. I lived in a one-bedroom apartment outside of Liberty City. The place was nothing extravagant while I prepared for the draft. My friends kept the place occupied more than me. In the meantime, I spent a lot of time working out at my old high school.

One day, I took out the time to visit Ms. Love's classroom. The girls screamed as I crept through the door. Ms. Love was shocked to see me.

I gave her a big hug. "Everybody, Ms. Love is my favorite teacher in the whole world."

Ms. Love smiled. "Thank you. You should tell them how important school is because some of them obviously don't get it," she said, throwing a hand on her hip. "That's why they're spending their summer with me."

A character in the back of the classroom tested me. "If school's so important, why you ain't finish?" he said, folding his arms like he was bad.

"First of all, I finished high school," I said. "Graduating high school is the biggest accomplishment in my life. If I had chosen to drop out or sell drugs I wouldn't be where I am today. School is very important; your future depends on it. I'm fortunate to be able to play basketball and make a good living, but even this isn't guaranteed."

A skinny, sloppy-dressed boy in the back of the classroom boldly asked, "What would you be if you wasn't a basketball player?"

"I'd be in school studying business so I could be a CEO of a Fortune 500 company . . ." I had the classroom at attention. It amazed me how much control I had over them.

The bell rang while I was talking. A couple of cats walked up to me and shook my hand. The tough character in the back walked past me with his head down. Ms. Love shook her head as he walked out the door. "I can't do anything with him; he's a lost cause." Then she sat on her desk and smiled at me. "I didn't know I was your favorite teacher in the whole world."

"Yes, if only you knew. I had the biggest crush on you."

"Please," she said, blowing it off lightly.

"I'm serious. You'd wear that long black skirt and walk down the aisle. Oh my God!"

She blushed. "Cut it out, you."

"Seriously."

She laughed. "So, how's life treating you?"

"Good. I'm looking forward to the draft."

"That's amazing. Don't forget about us."

"I'm here now, aren't I?"

"Yes, I have to give you credit for coming back because there are some athletes who forget about their communities."

"I'm gonna always come and give back. I feel like it's my responsibility."

"Please do because these kids need the support. Unfortunately, they won't listen to me, but they will listen to their favorite athlete or rapper . . ." Ms. Love's next class filed in.

"You know I'm down for the cause, Ms. Love." I gave her a hug goodbye, and then hit the weight room for a couple of hours.

* * *

After I finished working out, I went to my mother's house. The 600 Benz that I had given to her was parked in the driveway. My biggest dream was to buy my mother a house.

That evening, I took her on a ride to Coral Gables. We strolled through the suburbs looking at houses. There was a huge two-story house for sale. "Wow, I couldn't imagine living in something that big. I wouldn't know what to do with myself," she said.

I pulled up at the curb. "Well, you better figure it out real soon." I had spoken with the realtor a few days ago and made arrangements to see the property. Surprisingly, she pulled up in the driveway twenty minutes early.

"Come on, Momma," I said, getting out of the car.

"Jermaine, are you serious?"

"Yes, let's go check it out."

We took a look at the house and it was beautiful. It had 5 bedrooms, 4.5 bathrooms, and a big pool. The house sold for $1.2 million.

After we left the property, Momma began to cry.

"What's wrong?" I said.

"I can't believe it. God is good."

"Yes he is."

I took my mother to dinner. A few people took notice of me and began pointing. I didn't sweat it as I enjoyed dinner with Momma. Out of the blue, two slender busty women approached our table and sparked up a friendly conversation. After they left, Momma nodded her head. "Tramps."

"Momma, you don't even know those women."

"I know enough to tell that they're busy bodies. Please don't ever bring anything like that home," she said, buttering a roll.

"I got something to ask you, Momma."

"I'm listening."

"Here's the scenario: I asked Lindsey to move with me, but she claims she's not living with me unless we're married."

"I mean she isn't wrong."

"How come I knew you were gonna say that?" I dropped my salad fork because I had lost my appetite.

"'Cause you know better. Make sure you get a prenup."

"I'm not ready for marriage."

"You're young. Eventually you'll settle down and want to have children. I would love a couple grandbabies."

For a second, I pictured myself with a wife and kids. "I don't know."

"I would love to see you with a family instead of running the streets with lowlifes."

I hated when Momma badmouthed my friends. "I will never turn my back on the hood."

"You can save that ghetto-pride bullshit because I don't want to hear it. The bottom line is that you need to surround yourself with people who will look out for your best interest."

I let her have the last word as usual.

* * *

When I dropped Momma off home, Roy was sitting on the porch. "What's the deal with him?" I said.

"He talks about you all the time."

"For what?"

"He admires you. He's been working two jobs to pay you back."

"I don't want his money. I did it for you."

Momma gave me a hug then got out of the car. "Call me later," she said.

"Alright," I said, waving bye.

When Roy recognized me inside of the Chevy Camaro, he ran over. "How's it going, son?"

"I'm doing well."

"I'm proud of you."

I sighed because I didn't care to listen.

"Look, I know you don't wanna hear it, but I hope you find a place in your heart to forgive me. That's all I ask of you and nothing more. Okay?" he said, reaching out his hand.

I put the past behind us and shook his hand. Roy smiled and walked away as if I had made his day.

As I backed out the driveway, my phone rang. Bones was on the line. He told me that he needed to see me and it was an emergency.

"What's wrong?" I said.

"I can't talk over the phone."

"You're tripping. I'm on my way to the crib."

"Good, I'll meet you there soon."

I drove home in total suspense. When I pulled up to the building, Bones was waiting in his car. He got out of the Taurus and then hopped in my ride.

"What's going on?" I said.

"I need a big favor."

"What kind of favor?"

"I need you to loan me twenty thousand dollars."

"Twenty thousand dollars for what?"

"I found a connection."

I started laughing. "You're kidding, right?"

"I'm dead-ass serious. You don't see me laughing, do you? I'll pay you back."

"I don't have that kind of cash right now."

"Come on, I know you can make it happen. You know people that know people."

"Bro, I don't have it like everybody think I do. Contrary to what everybody may believe I'm broke until I officially sign a contract."

"You ain't gotta lie to me. Just say you don't wanna help a nigga out."

"I don't have to lie. It is what it is."

Bones hopped out of the car upset. "You ain't nothin' but a sellout!" he said, slamming the door.

I sat in the car while he vented.

"You've changed. You ain't shit, nigga!" he shouted at me.

Several kids riding through the complex on bicycles stopped to watch the action.

When Bones kicked the passenger's side door, I got out of the car. "You need to chill out!" I said.

"Fuck you!" he said. Then he got in his car and swerved off down the street.

I went upstairs and refused to lose sleep.

* * *

I received a call from the Houston Rockets. I was flown into town for a workout. When I got there, I stayed at one of the finest hotels. I was treated like a star. The Houston Rockets was definitely a first-class organization.

After spending a couple of days in Houston, I wouldn't have minded playing alongside one of the best big men in the game, Yao Ming. The workout went excellent. Everyone was hopeful that if the chips fell in place, I'd be a Houston Rocket.

When I got back to Miami, I received a call from White Chocolate. We hadn't spoken in months but we talked as if we hadn't skipped a beat. My pal wanted to paint the town red and I was all for it.

Late that night, we ended up at Tootsie's Cabaret. We had the time of our lives. I paid for a few lap dances then played stingy for the rest of the night. White Chocolate was hooked. I watched him spend all his money. I had to drag him out of the place.

When I walked out the club, I saw Deion in the parking lot. I got nervous because he had a bunch of dudes with him and I didn't want any trouble. He approached me with his entourage.

White Chocolate and I were cornered. I thought it was going down.

Deion folded his arms and stepped to me. "I see you. Keep it up, cousin-in-law," he said, holding out his hand. We shook hands as if to squash the beef.

"Believe that, bro," I said, shocked.

After they left, I took a deep breath, and got in the car.

* * *

White Chocolate dropped me off home. I walked up the flight of stairs, then through the hallway to my apartment. The door was cracked open as if someone had been inside. I kicked open the door and hit on the light switch. All of my things were scattered over the place. I stepped over everything and slowly walked through the apartment. My mattress was turned over and my dresser drawers were emptied. I checked the closet and it had been ransacked too. My jewelry was missing from its secret hiding place in the closet. I was mad as I stormed out the front door. A gang of kids was standing in the parking lot. I ran downstairs and approached them. "Hey, did y'all see anyone go inside my apartment?"

"Nope," one said, shrugging.

I looked all six of them in the eye to see if they were lying. "No one saw anything?"

"No," they all said.

"Sure y'all didn't," I said, unconvinced.

I walked the entire apartment building looking for a guilty face. After harassing everybody in sight, I went back to my apartment. I slammed the door and plopped on the couch. I started thinking to myself: *a brother can't have nothing in the hood.*

25

THE NEXT MORNING, I CLEANED up my apartment. It took me forever to put the place back together. For hours, I sat on the couch curling my fingers around two metal stress balls. I was mad at the world. My phone kept ringing but I didn't feel up to talking to a soul.

After I thought over the whole situation, I couldn't sit back and let it go. I got up and hit the streets. There was no way I could sleep another night without protection.

I bought a semi-automatic pistol from a friend of Chance's. As I drove Chance back home, he started digging for information. "Who do you think did it?"

"I have no clue but if I find out, it's on."

"I'ont blame you."

"It's a shame. I can't even live around my own peoples because they're trifling."

"That's true. They feel like if they don't have shit then why should you?"

"We're like crabs in a bucket," I said, shaking my head.

I dropped Chance off home and then headed to Gold's Gym to work out with Brandon. Amid the chaos, Lindsey was on my mind. I hadn't talked to her in weeks ever since we disagreed on marriage. Usually, she was the one I could turn to in the time of stress and confusion.

I started to pick up the phone and call, but my ego was too big. Instead I called my squeeze, Angelina. I needed balance in my life. I was tired of confiding in my homies. After all, I was beginning to realize those cats were only out for themselves.

When I got to the gym, Brandon had started working out without me. He was sweating bullets as he leg-pressed. A couple of in-shape hotties had him surrounded.

I walked over and butted in. "You ain't have to wait on me, bro."

Brandon smiled and put the brakes on his workout. "What's good, my dude? I didn't think you were coming."

"It's all good," I said, placing down my bag on the floor. Then I stretched.

Brandon started talking about the draft. He was excited upon getting the opportunity to work out for the Knicks. "I'm feeling New York. That city is amazing. I mean, you go there and it's like what dreams are made of, man. Working out inside of Madison Square Garden gave me chills."

"Watch you end up in Toronto."

"Why you trying to jinx me?"

"I'm just saying. I'd hate to see you get your hopes all high and whatnot."

"Right," he sighed.

The two girls lingered around us while we worked out. They were very pleasant and friendly. They had Brandon and I rolling. A heavy, pasty-colored guy shook his head as we goofed off like four clowns. His body was full of tattoos and piercings.

"Is that your man?" I asked one of the girls jokingly.

They burst out laughing. "No way," the voluptuous one said.

"That cat sure looking over here like he's gotta problem."

Time slipped away while we worked out and had fun. Nighttime crept up and it started drizzling. I was hungry and eager to go before the rain came down harder. Brandon and I grabbed our things and headed for the door. The two girls waved goodbye to us as we walked across the parking lot.

"Alright, Brandon, I'll check you later," I said.

We split up.

I maneuvered between parked cars to get to my ride. The rain started coming down hard. As I tipped across the parking lot, a truck sped towards me. I jumped out the way before it hit me. "Stupid, motherfucker!" I said.

They stomped on brakes and reversed. Next thing I know, I was standing face to face with a double-barrel shotgun. My heart was beating fast as the fat guy from inside Gold's Gym stared me in the eye.

"Fucking, monkey! Stay with your own kind," he said, speeding off like a coward.

I shook my head and kept walking. It upset me that people still couldn't see past color.

When I got in the car, my phone started ringing. Chance was going bananas.

"Guess who got busted," he said.

"Who?"

"Louie."

The news took me by surprise. "Are you for real?" I said.

"If I'm lying, I'm flying. They caught him on his way out of the country to Santo Domingo."

"That's too bad."

"At least he went out on top."

At that moment, I thanked God that I never fell into the trap of selling drugs.

* * *

Every night, I slept with protection within arm's reach. I slept like a baby because my pistol was a guardian angel.

When I woke up this morning, Angelina's head was lying on my chest. I would've liked to've slept in, but I had a busy morning ahead of me. I vowed that I'd make a guest appearance on Sun Sports TV. Even though I was tired from a busy week of traveling, I couldn't back out.

When I got out the shower, Angelina was awake. I started getting dressed.

"Where are you going?" she said.

"I have a show to do; I'll be back. Just call me if you need me." I put on my shoes and then headed out the door.

When I got to the television studio, I was greeted like a star. The producer informed me that I'd be on in fifteen minutes. I was a bit nervous because it was my first appearance on a live show.

A lovely dark-skinned sister came towards me with a make-up sponge. "Come, handsome," she said.

I backed away. "I don't do make-up," I said.

She started laughing. "It's not make-up. It's only a sponge to take away the shine, sweetie."

"Oh, alright."

"Five minutes," someone yelled.

She fixed my collar and smiled. "Go get 'em."

At commercial break, I walked on the set. I met two of the local TV sports announcers that I grew up watching. It seemed weird being on this side of the television screen. I gathered myself together when the producer shouted we were on.

"First and foremost, Jermaine Parker, we would like to thank you for coming on the show ... ladies and gentleman we are pleased to have our hometown hero in the studio today," Dan said, smiling.

I smiled back. "Thank you guys for having me."

"Jermaine, what does it feel like to be in your shoes? We're talking about the most coveted player in the NBA draft?" Patrick said, creating a feeling of excitement.

"It's been a rollercoaster ride, you know. I'm a bit anxious, like everyone else is to find out where I'll end up."

"Where'd you like to jumpstart your career?" he said.

"I'd be honored to be a part of any team in the NBA. I had the opportunity to work out for Houston, New Jersey, and the Clippers. It was a bit nerve racking but fun."

"Which organization stuck out the most?" Dan said.

"Honestly I was impressed with all of them."

"Could you see yourself staying in South Florida and playing for Coach Spoelstra and the Heat?" Patrick said.

"Although it sounds good, it'd be wishful thinking ..."

The questions kept coming. After we returned from commercial break, I felt a bit more comfortable. We started talking about my short-lived career at the University of Florida. My highlight reel rolled across the television screen.

"Do you miss Gator basketball?" Dan said.

"Of course I do. We had a very special team. Shout out to all those guys, man. I thought we could've done a lot of great things, but unfortunately it didn't happen that way."

"Why not stay and give it another go?" he said.

"Trust me I'd thought about it."

"What'd you want to say to all the Gator fans out there?"

"The money made me do it; I'm sorry," I said, wiping away imaginary tears.

Dan and Patrick started laughing hysterically. "Can you blame the kid?" Dan said.

"Not at all," Patrick said.

"Who's your pick to win the NBA finals?" Dan asked.

"I have to go with the defending champs. They're looking really good," I said.

Time rolled by quickly as we talked sports and had fun. After I finished the TV show, I was escorted out of the building with security. A small crowd of people was gathered outside at the gate. They waved and cheered for me. I got inside of my car and rode away, feeling humbled.

* * *

When I got home, I turned off my phone and slept like a baby. I was exhausted, but when I woke up I felt like the Energizer Bunny.

Angelina begged me to take her out on the town because she was tired of sitting inside.

"No," I said.

"Why not?"

"I have my reasons."

"Are you afraid of the paparazzi?"

"It's not even that kind of party."

"Fine, I'll catch a cab."

I cracked up. "You must don't know you're in the hood, girl."

Angelina and I ended up at the mall. Dudes were checking her out because she was fly. I put my arm around her shoulders. A couple of sisters seemed unimpressed as we walked the mall. I could read the expression on their faces.

I saw Nia in the Footlocker with a big round belly. She saw me too and approached me while I looked for sneakers. "Hey, Jermaine," she said.

"What's good, Nia?"

"I wish I could lie and tell you life is sweet." She put her head down. "I'm making it but it's hard."

I felt bad for Nia because Louie had knocked her up.

"As you know Louie is locked up and I'm pregnant with his baby . . ."

Angelina walked over and handed me a box of shoes. "Here you go, pappy," she said.

"Thank you." I sat down and tried them on while Nia hung around. "Well, it was nice seeing you," I said.

"You too."

I stood up and gave her a hug. "Keep your head up," I whispered.

"I'm trying, Jermaine. You just don't know how hard it is, boo." She had tears in her eyes.

I figured Nia knew she had passed up on a good thing.

After shopping at the Footlocker, Angelina lured me into Prada. The price tags were on the hefty side. She had picked out three dresses, which rang up to $890 at the counter. Angelina was short by $160. She looked at me.

"Don't look at me," I said.

The lady at the register smiled. "All the items are on sale, sir."

"Please," Angelina begged me.

I handed the cashier the rest of the money. Then Angelina wrapped her arms around me.

"Thank you," she said.

"You can thank me later."

"Can't wait," she said, kissing me.

* * *

We had dinner inside of the mall at the Grand Lux Cafe. Two gentlemen noticed me and stopped at our table. They were UF alumni. "Dude, you're amazing! We're really going to miss you. Any chance of you coming back?" the short one said.

I was tired of people asking me the same question. "I don't think so."

"That sucks."

"I'd take the money too," the tall one said

I wiped off my mouth. "Oh, without a doubt."

"You're still my favorite player and I wish you luck," the short one said.

"Thank you."

After they left, I called the waitress for the tab. I placed $70 on the table. Then we walked out of the restaurant. Angelina wrapped her arms around me. Surprisingly, Coach Baxter and his wife met us on the way out.

My heart sped up.

"Jermaine, what a surprise," Coach Baxter said.

"Hey, Coach," I said.

"How's it going?"

"Good," I said.

"That's great." He reached his hand out to Angelina. "Your name?"

"Angelina."

"I'm his high school coach. I taught him everything he knows, right?"

Everyone started laughing.

"Right," I said.

"Honey, do you know where Ethan and Lindsey ran off too? Today's Susan's birthday."

"Happy birthday," I said.

Mrs. Baxter smiled. "Thank you."

Lindsey and Ethan walked over.

I wanted to get away.

Lindsey looked at me as if she couldn't believe her eyes. "You frigging jerk!" she yelled, slapping me. She'd smacked me so hard that I couldn't feel my face. Then she ran away crying. Ethan and Mrs. Baxter took off behind her.

Everyone looked shocked.

Coach Baxter turned and looked at me as if he were possessed. "Are you fucking my daughter?"

"No, sir."

"Stay away from her," he said, walking away.

I looked at Angelina and shook my head. "Thanks," I said.

* * *

When I got home, someone had broken into my apartment again. The doorknob was on the ground. "Damn, not again!" I said.

"Ay yi yi," Angelina said.

I gave her the keys to the car. "Go sit in the car and wait for me."

She rushed downstairs and got in the car.

When I checked through the apartment, my gun was missing. That was the only thing of value that I had in my apartment. But that still didn't ease the fact that someone had violated me.

I walked outside and looked over the balcony. There were two boys standing in the street tossing a football. I ran downstairs and took the ball away. "How long have y'all been outside?" I said.

"Why?" the slim boy said.

I grabbed his throat. "Don't ask me why, punk."

"Get off me! You ain't nobody, nigga."

"I'm gonna ask you again: how long have you been outside?" I said, tightening my grip on his throat.

"Since six o'clock. Now let me go!"

I let him ago. "Did any one of y'all see someone go inside of my apartment?"

"I ain't no snitch. Snitches get stitches."

I grabbed him again. "I'm running out of patience. Don't make me beat your li'l skinny ass! Now I'm gonna ask you again, did you see anybody go inside of my apartment?"

He folded his arms stubbornly. "I ain't tellin' you shit."

I snapped and punched him in the mouth. "You think I'm playing with your stupid ass?"

He spat out blood.

The chubby boy was shaking. "Just tell him."

"Okay," he said. "It was you know – that dude with the dreads that you was outside arguing with one day . . ."

Immediately, Bones came to mind. I let go of the kid and fixed his shirt. "I appreciate it. Go clean yourself up," I said, handing him a few dollars.

"Thanks!" he smiled, bloody-lipped.

I jumped in my car and sped away.

* * *

That night, I checked Angelina into a hotel. As I helped her get settled into the room, I called Chance and told him what had happened. He was ready to roll. I grabbed my keys off the dresser and headed for the door.

Angelina sat on the bed, looking confused. "What about me?" she said.

"I'll be back."

"Is everything okay?"

"Of course. Just wait here for me, okay?"

I sped over to Chance's crib. He got in the car with a pistol on his waist. "Let's ride," he said, putting on his shades like *The Terminator*.

We rode the streets looking for Bones. For a straight hour, we stayed on a mission. "There he is!" Chance said. He'd spotted him coming outside of a hole-in-the-wall club.

I watched Bones from a distance as traffic moved across the parking lot slowly. People kept blocking my view. I was hoping we didn't lose him.

"What are we waiting for? Let's get him!" Chance said.

"No, chill out. I know what I'm doing."

A patrol car strolled through the parking lot on duty.

"See what I'm saying?" I pointed.

Bones and one of his partners got into a white Mitsubishi Galant. They drove out of the parking lot and headed south. I followed them four miles and ended up to a liquor store. Bones and his partner got out of the car and walked across the parking lot.

"Let's get him," Chance said, loading a clip into his nine-millimeter.

I reached for the gun. "Let me handle this."

Chance handed me the pistol. "Do your thing," he said.

We both got out of the car and ran across the half-lit parking lot. We hid between two cars and waited for them to come out of the store. "Here they come," Chance said, peeping up.

I could hear them getting closer.

Bones approached the passenger's side. I hopped up and scared the crap out of him. His bottle of alcohol hit the ground. He looked startled. "What the fuck is goin' on?" he said.

I held the gun to his temple. "You know what's up!"

"I'ont know shit."

Immediately, I spotted my jewelry. "That bling around your neck and wrist looks like it belongs to me. Man, take it off!" I said.

He took off the jewelry and placed it in my hand.

"Fucking snake," I said.

"Shoot him," Chance said.

"Yeah shoot me, pussy."

"Hell, I'll do it. Give me the gun," Chance said.

"Chill," I said, backing away with the gun aimed at Bones' forehead. Bones made a move like I was bluffing. I fired the gun through the car window and he froze. Then I hopped in my car and took off before we got caught. "Can you believe that cat? There ain't nothing worse than a thief," I said, handing the gun to Chance.

"No, keep it. You never know; you may need it."

"Good looking out." I set the gun in my glove compartment.

"You got to watch who you break bread with, money."

"Tell me about it."

It hurt me that my own peoples would steal from me. I didn't know who I could trust.

* * *

After I dropped off Chance, I headed back to the hotel. Angelina was asleep. I crawled in bed and laid down. It had been a long hectic day and pulling a gun on Bones didn't make it any better.

My phone rang in the middle of the night. I picked up.

"Why'd you pull a gun on Bones?" Floyd shouted through the phone.

"Look, man, don't call my phone with that bullshit," I said, hanging up.

Floyd called back. "Don't come back to Liberty City or you dead, mothafucka!" he said, hanging up on me.

I knew that I had stirred up drama and I had to face it.

2 6

Two weeks later, I moved to a luxurious two-bedroom apartment in an upscale neighborhood. The rent was $1600 a month but Scott had no problem with furnishing me with the best. Finally, I'd come to the realization that I couldn't live around my own people. There were too many of us starving in the hood. My safety was a concern for the people who cared for me. All the same, it hurt to have cats I had grown up with turn on me because of money. Chance and I had fallen out in a matter of days over money too. He was griping because I wouldn't help him finance his dog-fighting business. Having money and success wasn't as fun as I thought it would be.

When I got back in town from L.A., the place was a mess. The dishes were piled up to the ceiling. Angelina was on the phone running her mouth. I was tired of her laziness. On top of that, she couldn't cook worth shit. All she wanted to do was sit around and look pretty all day.

I took a shower and then laid in bed because I was tired. I had spent two days in L.A. on a business trip. Converse was interested in marketing me as a brand. I left my options open although their presentation was enticing.

Angelina came in the room and laid beside me. She started kissing on me and rubbing my chest.

I grabbed her hand before it slid down my drawers. "You have got to go," I said.

"What?"

"Get your things."

She sat up and looked at me. "What is your problem?"

"Just do what I said." I got up and put on some clothes.

"I'm sorry," she said

"Yes me too. I didn't mean to lead you on this way."

After she packed her things, I took her to rent a car and then went about my business.

* * *

When I got home, I found myself staring at the walls. I couldn't take the boredom so I called my homie.

That night, Kevin and I hit the gentleman's club. We had a good time watching some of the most beautiful women in the world entertain us. I spent countless hours throwing away cash on girls. After blowing $5,000 on strippers, Kevin forced me out of the club.

As Kevin and I walked out of the strip club, two masked gunmen approached us. They made us lay on the ground and robbed us at gunpoint.

I handed over my jewelry and wallet.

One of them reached down to the ground and picked up our belongings. I recognized Bones' scarred left thumb. "Man, why are you doing this?" I said.

Kevin started begging for his life as they held pistols to our heads. I didn't panic because I didn't believe that Bones was man enough to kill us. Suddenly, one of them pulled the trigger and ran. I was in shock as Kevin lay on the ground with a great-big hole in the back of his head. "Please, God!" I cried, grabbing his stiff body.

When the police arrived on the scene, I hadn't moved. I remained on the ground covered in my friend's blood. I couldn't believe Kevin was gone.

* * *

The media ran with the story all week. My name was the gossip of every news station and the subject matter of every newspaper in the country. The *Miami Herald, Sun Sentinel,* and *New York Post* wrote the most garbage. ESPN covered the story and made me look like the bad guy. One night, Charles Barkley bashed me, too, while covering the NBA playoffs on TNT. It seemed like everyone was insensitive to my situation when they learned that I was a part of an ongoing investigation.

On the night of the shooting, detectives had brought me in for questioning. They wanted to know if I had any involvement leading up to the homicide. I didn't cooperate. That following day, I had hired a high-powered attorney. He assured me that I was in good hands but I was still nervous. Every day I prayed that my troubles didn't interfere with me getting drafted.

Two weeks after the shooting, I identified Bones in the lineup. It was the hardest thing I ever had to do in my life. I almost cried on my way out of the jail. When I walked outside, WSVN and CBS News station was staked out in the parking lot. It seemed like the more money, the more problems. I dodged the news reporters and got in the car with my mother. She was visibly upset at the media for attacking me. "Get a life!" she shouted as I got in the car.

We eased out the parking lot away from all the chaos. Momma looked at me. "Are you all right?"

"Why me?"

"You have to be strong. You're going to get through this, baby."

I turned the radio to 960 Sports Talk. As expected, I was the topic of the hour. "When are these players going to stand up and take responsibility for their actions?" the radio host said.

A caller phoned in. "What is it with athletes and strip joints? I mean, really, dude, I think every GM needs to put a clause in their contracts that reads no titty bars."

The host laughed. "Imagine that, Joey. That scenario screams lockout!"

Another caller phoned in. "I think the problem is you give these guys all this money and fame without any consequences. For crying out loud, Pac Man Jones is a prime example. He could do no wrong in the eyes of Jerry Jones. Somewhere these owners have to draw the line."

The next caller phoned in. "They're kids with a lot of money who've never had anything. What does everyone expect? Here's one to remember: you can take the boy out of the ghetto, but you can't take the ghetto out of the boy."

A brother called in and defended me. "Y'all are treating this young man like a criminal when he was the victim. I agree that when you reach a certain status you can't do the same things or hang out the same places you used to hang; but still all in the same, he was the victim of a robbery."

Another caller phoned in. "Blah blah at he's a victim. He's an egotistical bastard. He couldn't stay out of trouble at the University of Florida and now some team will be stupid enough to pay this creep millions of dollars. What a crock of shit!"

"Please watch your language. Profanity will not be tolerated –"

Momma turned off the radio. "That's the kind of mess you don't need in your ear. Those people don't know you, Jermaine."

When I got home, after dropping off Momma, I broke down. I sat in the living room in complete darkness crying my eyes out. All day I'd walked around trying to hide the pain until I couldn't take it no more. I was hurting. Identifying Bones in the lineup was equally as hard as preparing to attend Kevin's funeral next week. My life felt like a nightmare. I kept wishing I'd wake up.

* * *

I met with my attorney and he delighted me with good news. My name was cleared from any further investigation. I thanked God because I could get on with my life and grieve the loss of my best friend in peace. Although things worked out in my favor, I knew it wouldn't sit well with a lot of cats in the hood that I had ratted out Bones.

One morning while walking out of my attorney's office, the media rushed me. My attorney spoke on my behalf.

"Can you give us the ramifications of this ongoing investigation involving Mr. Parker?" a CBS News reporter asked.

"The investigation has been dropped . . . my client is cleared from any wrongdoing . . . he was a victim of a heinous crime and the suspects will be brought to justice . . ."

The pack of reporters trailed me to my mother's car. I looked professional for the cameras in a black suit and tie. Image meant everything to me at this point. I got in the car and gave Momma a big hug. "Thank you for being there for me, Momma."

She patted me on the back. "You're my baby."

Momma and I went to breakfast and then spent most of the day at Granny's.

* * *

When I got home that evening, there was a feeling of emptiness inside of me. I tried to force myself not to think about Bones or the death of my friend, but it was impossible not to. Brandon called me and gave me his condolences. We stayed on the phone for a moment and chatted about the upcoming draft, too. I anticipated that big day and so did he. Next month couldn't come fast enough for us. All I thought about was moving my mother out of the slums. I only prayed that teams wouldn't overlook me because of my recent troubles.

After we got off the phone, a lonely feeling came over me. I let go of my pride and called Lindsey. The phone rang until her voicemail picked up. I left a sweet message and she called back. When I heard her voice, it made me happy. "I miss you so much," I said.

Lindsey sat on the phone in complete silence, while I poured out my heart.

"My life has been a mess without you," I admitted. "Can you please come over? I can't be in this place alone. I feel like I'm losing it, yo."

Lindsey didn't decline my invitation. I gave her directions and then got off my butt. I straightened up the place because it was a mess. After I finished cleaning up, I turned off the lights. The moonlight cast a bright shadow in the living room. I relaxed on the couch hoping she wouldn't let me down.

When I heard a knock at the door, I got up and opened it. Lindsey walked in and stood at the door.

"I don't bite," I said, giving her a big hug. Then I walked in the living room and sat down.

Lindsey followed me and sat at the opposite end of the couch. "Nice place," she said.

"Thanks. Is there a reason for this huge space between us?" I said.

"Jermaine, why did you call me over here when it's obvious I'm not good enough for you?"

"That's not true. I love you." I closed the gap between us. "I know your father hates me."

"Do you blame him?"

"No, that's why I have to fix this mess. Maybe I can come over for dinner one night?"

"I don't think that would be a good idea."

"You hate me too, don't you?"

"I don't know."

"I think if you really did, you wouldn't be here."

"Truthfully, I don't know why I'm here."

"I hope you're here because you love me." I kissed her on the cheek. "Look me in the eye and tell me you don't love me so we can turn the page."

Lindsey couldn't look me in the eye. "No, I can't," she said, crying.

I got down on my knees and placed her arms around me. We started kissing and the touch of her lips drove me wild. She gave me a feeling that no other woman could match. I wanted her so bad that the pain in my stomach wouldn't go away.

We ended up dry humping on the couch because she didn't wanna go all the way. Once again, I respected her decision to remain abstinent although I was about to die of deprivation.

I lay on the couch with her wrapped inside of my arms, craving her body.

"I love you," she said, kissing me on the cheek.

"If you loved me you wouldn't make me suffer."

"Love is pain."

"You ain't never lied," I said, rubbing her back. "I need you to come with me to a funeral this weekend."

The room went silent for a second. "Okay," she agreed.

I shook my head. "I can't get it out of my mind. I watched Kevin beg for his life and then all of a sudden they pulled the trigger." My sinuses started acting up and I began sniffling.

"It's going to be okay," she said.

"Then I think to myself, what if it was me?"

Lindsey rubbed her hand across my chest. "I'd die without you."

I knew she meant it too. Suddenly, I built up the nerve to pop the big question. "Will you marry me?"

Lindsey sat up and looked at me as if I were joking. "Are you serious, Jermaine? Please don't play with my emotions."

"Yes, I'm serious. Will you marry me?"

"Yes!" she said, bouncing on top of me, excited.

I felt it was right

* * *

The funeral was held at New Birth Baptist Church on a dark and rainy Saturday afternoon. The church was filled from the floor to the balcony. Almost every row was filled with ball players. There was no doubt that many people loved Kevin.

Everyone was drenched in tears as the eulogy was read. Kevin's older sister, Charmaine, did her best to comfort their mother. I sat in the third row with my head down, crying. The pain was unbearable. Lindsey kept her arms around me, trying to hold me together.

After the eulogy, Bishop Wright began preaching. His sermon touched everybody as he yelled. "Weeping may endure for a night, but joy cometh in the morning! Young men, God is speaking to you," he said, looking into some of our teary eyes. "Let him into your hearts before it's too late."

At the cemetery, I sat beside Ms. Smith at her request. She held my hand tightly as Kevin was lowered into the ground.

I wrapped my arms around her and did my best to hold up. It was tough.

* * *

Life had to carry on. Two weeks later, I was back into the normal routine of life. As the draft neared, a tentative workout schedule kept me busy and out of trouble. Then on Sundays, I found myself in church.

This Sunday, I was sharply dressed in a dark blue suit. I had my Bible in hand as I listened to the word of God.

Bishop Wright made Brandon and I stand up. "Look how God works!" he said.

Everyone started clapping and started shouting, "Hallelujah!"

"He's not through yet. You gentleman may have a seat. Praise God for these young brothers," he said.

After church was dismissed, the women were aggressive at introducing themselves. It shocked me. One girl named Sonya gave me her number. She was a cutie with hazel eyes and a nice womanly shape. We talked and then exchanged numbers.

"Nice meeting you," I said.

She smiled. "Nice meeting you too. Call me."

"Okay." I got inside of Brandon's pearl white Range Rover and watched her twist across the parking lot. "Lord, help me." I sighed.

"What happened?"

"That was the preacher's daughter."

Brandon laughed. "Don't do it."

"I'm not," I said, ripping her number to shreds.

* * *

After Brandon took me home, I drove over to Lindsey's house. She had invited me over for dinner to announce our plans of getting married. I was a bit nervous to show my face. Lindsey had persuaded me that everyone was cool though. When I got to her house, it didn't seem that way. Coach Baxter never said a word to me, as he and I sat in the living room watching the Lakers-Thunder playoff series.

During halftime, I dug up the strength to ask him the big question. "Coach Baxter, I need to ask you a very important question." There was a dry lump in my throat.

"Go right ahead."

I cleared my throat. "I would like to know if I could have your daughter's hand in marriage."

He paused and then stood up over me. I thought he was gonna kill me.

"You two have my blessings," he smiled.

I stood up and he hugged me tightly. "Thank you so much," I said.

"You better take good care of my daughter."

"I will."

Coach Baxter made the announcement at the dinner table.

Mrs. Baxter started crying. "Congratulations!" she said.

I smiled at Lindsey, happy at the fact that everything panned out smoothly.

* * *

That same night when I told my mother, she was disappointed. Although she didn't wanna see me tie the knot to a white woman, she gave us her blessings. "Prenup," she repeated through the telephone.

After I hung up with my nagging mother, I sat on my bed in deep thought. I'd thought it over and I remained optimistic about marrying my high school girlfriend. After all, she was there for me from the beginning.

The following weekend, I officially proposed to Lindsey on the balcony of my apartment, overlooking the city. The view of the sunset was out of this world. I slid a two-karat VVS stone on her finger. Her eyes sparkled like the huge rock on her hand. All of a sudden, she hugged me and started crying.

"Why are you crying?" I said.

"I can't believe it."

"I love you, girl. You're my everything."

* * *

Lindsey, Brandon, Sherri, and I ate at Prime 112 on a crowded night. ESPN had a cam in the spot as we tuned into the NBA playoffs and the NBA draft lottery. All night, the cameras hovered around our table while adoring fans cheered in the background. I was the focus of attention. An ESPN reporter asked me for my take on the draft. I gave my opinion and then tuned into the draft.

New Jersey won the draft lottery. The team chairman of the Nets announced that his team would select 7'2" center, Andrew Miller, out of Wake Forest. Everyone booed New Jersey's selection.

I felt betrayed.

"That's a big shock," Brandon said.

I was nervous and upset after things didn't go as I had expected. My phone started blowing up but I didn't pick up.

"Can you believe they selected that sorry white boy with the first pick? What a waste," Brandon said, shaking his head. Brandon's mulatto girlfriend, Sherri, shook her head.

"Would it have been better if he were black?" she said.

"No, it would've been better if he were somebody with some goddamn talent; I see Darko Milicic all over again."

I tried not to let the disappointment show on my face. "They had the right to pick who they wanted, so let it go," I said, playing the good-sport role.

Milwaukee and Toronto came in second and third on the board.

"Oh hell," Brandon said, licking sauce off his fingers. "Milwaukee?"

"What's wrong with Milwaukee?" Sherri said.

"Would you like to live in Milwaukee? I mean, come on, what the hell is in Wisconsin other than some goddamn cheese?"

"Wisconsin is beautiful," Lindsey said.

"You've been there before?" I said.

"Yes."

"Well alright then."

Fifteen minutes later, Scott rang my phone and calmed my nerves. "Hang in there, Jermaine," he told me.

At that point, I didn't care where I ended. Getting drafted was my main concern.

After I hung up with Scott, Brandon asked me, "What's up?"

"That was Scott. He was a bit shocked at New Jersey's pick."

"I told you."

"I want it to be over, bro. The suspense is driving me crazy. I'm ready to move on and start my life in a different place." *I meant it too*. I was tired of having to watch my back. My name was the talk of the streets in Miami. Several times, I had received death threats that I couldn't come back to Liberty City because I was labeled a snitch. To add fuel to the fire, I was considered a sellout because I had moved away from the hood. It was plain to see that my success brought on a lot of hate. The burden of it all was heavy on my shoulders. Occasionally, I'd smoke weed to relieve the stress. Sometimes, I felt like all the money in the world wasn't worth the problems. Life seemed simpler when I had less.

"Draft day I'm going to rock a lime-green pimp suit," Brandon said.

I burst out laughing.

"No you aren't and you ain't no pimp. Get it right," Sherri said.

"Will you hush?"

The waitress brought the ticket and walked away in tiny shorts. She was a hottie. Brandon got in trouble for looking at her butt.

"You want her now?" Sherri snapped.

"What are you talking about? See what I go through y'all?"

"You're not the only one," I said.

"At least try and play it off, you know what I'm saying?" she said.

Lindsey jumped on her side. "Exactly."

"Have faith in your man," Brandon said.

"Yeah right," Lindsey and Sherri both said.

I looked at Lindsey. "What'd you mean, yeah right? Why would you marry someone you don't trust?"

"You can love somebody and not trust them. Duh," Sherri said.

"It's not supposed to be that way." I looked at Lindsey. "If you don't trust me then you need to let me know right now."

"Let's get off this, please. Y'all getting too serious," Brandon said.

I tossed the money on the table for the waitress. Then I got up and walked out of the restaurant. A handful of people bombarded me for autographs. I signed all the ones I could. More people trotted my way and I shook my head. "That's it, people. I'm so sorry; I have to go," I said.

Brandon walked outside and caught up with me. "You cool?" he said.

"Yeah."

"No you ain't."

We headed across the parking lot to get away from the ruckus.

"I want you to spend forty thousand dollars on a woman who tells you she doesn't trusts you," I said, shaking my head.

"I feel you on that one."

Lindsey and Sherri walked out of the restaurant.

"Alright, homie. Handle your business," Brandon said, walking towards his truck.

Sherri and Lindsey stood in the parking lot talking. I got in my car and flashed the high beams. "Will you come on?" I said.

Lindsey came and got in the car. "What is with you?"

"You really don't trust me?"

"I think you're blowing the whole thing out of proportion. I never said I didn't trust you."

"You insinuated it. I can't give you my all if you don't trust me."

"I trust you."

"You better mean it too."

"Oh so now you don't trust me?"

"Yes, I trust you – that's why I want you to be my wife."

* * *

June 22, I sat inside of a packed Madison Square Garden Arena on edge. The media was heavily on hand. I was nervous. All week, I had been anxious to see where the cards would fall. Lindsey and my mother were seated beside me. I waited patiently as the commissioner took the stage and announced the first draft pick of the New Jersey Nets, Andrew Miller. The crowd at Madison Square Garden gave him a lukewarm ovation. He posed for the camera with his team cap and jersey in hand. After the selection, the commissioner prepared to announce the second pick. "With the second pick of the NBA draft, the Milwaukee Bucks select Eugene Watson ..."

I was burning up inside but I didn't let it show.

After Eugene left the platform, the commissioner prepared to announce the third pick, which belonged to Houston. "With the third pick of the NBA draft, the Houston Rockets select Nathaniel Evans ..."

After I had slipped down in the draft, I began having doubts about leaving school early. The commissioner was given the go ahead for the fourth selection. "With the fourth pick of the NBA draft, the Los Angeles Clippers select Jermaine Parker out of the University of Florida ..."

I heard a lot of cheers. My heart was racing in excitement. I stood up and hugged my mother. She was in tears. Then I hugged Lindsey. It felt like a dream come true.

I walked on stage with a big smile on my face. The commissioner shook my hand. Then he handed me a team cap and jersey. I slid on my cap and held my new team's jersey in hand as the cameras flashed.

The commissioner looked at me. "Congratulations, Mr. Parker."

"Thank you, sir."

It was a day I could never forget.

27

I SIGNED A THREE-YEAR DEAL worth 8.9 million dollars. Most of the money I received came from endorsements. I agreed to a five-million-dollar deal with Converse. I was the face of Converse for the next three years. I had a lot of offers on the table. Scott was in the process of negotiating a two-million-dollar deal with Under Armour. Money was flowing in from everywhere. It was hard to get a grip.

I bought my mother a nice five-bedroom home in Coral Gables totaling $1.2 million. I felt it was well deserved. Then Lindsey and I moved into a four-bedroom house in Cutler Bay, which was dope enough to be featured on *MTV Cribs*. Lindsey and I threw a party almost every other weekend. There was never a dull night in the neighborhood. A few times, the neighbors had called the police on us but that didn't stop us from partying. It was a dream come true to have a place I could call my home. Every night, I would get down on my knees and thank God.

I tried to get my grandmother out of the slums of Opa-Locka, but she refused to leave her house. The rest of the family wasn't so modest. My uncle Gary constantly threw investment deals at me while Roy begged me to start a carpet and tile business. Aunties, uncles, cousins, nieces, and nephews that I didn't know came out of the woodwork. I was slowly learning that the more money I had, the more misery it brought. I had everyone calling me for favors. It never ended. Friends that I went to school with had their hands out too. With every no, came more enemies. It was hard on me. Sometimes I would lay awake in the middle of the night stressed out. All the pressure and hate made me uneasy. On several occasions, I'd thought of hiring a bodyguard. One night, I had someone follow me halfway home until I turned into a police station. That night, I could've flashed my pistol as a warning but I didn't need the headache. I had to keep my composure although it was tough.

When I woke up this morning, my Range Rover was sitting in the driveway on its rotors. Someone had stolen the rims and tires. Immediately, I reported it.

The next day, the *Sun Sentinel* and *Miami Herald* had the story in the paper. I hated that my life was everybody else's entertainment.

That same day, my mother called me back-to-back while I was in the middle of a meeting with Scott. We discussed a possible two-million-dollar deal involving Under Armour over lunch at Benihana's. I was all for it.

After several interruptions, I picked up the phone.

Momma sounded upset. "Is everything all right?" she said.

"Yes, mother. Everything's cool."

"Are you sure? When I got the news I thought somebody got hurt."

"No, everybody's okay. I'll call you back later," I said, hanging up."

Scott and I continued our discussion. "Can we please try and reach a deal before the mid part of July? I wanna go into summer league with my mind clear and focused," I said.

"I absolutely agree. I'll try and arrange a meeting this week, so you can get familiar with the company."

"Make it happen."

"Slow down. We don't need to bite off more than we can chew. What are your scheduled dates and times for the commercial shoot with Converse?"

"This week Thursday and Friday."

"Great then we'll arrange the meeting for next week. Sounds good?"

"Make sure it's not on Thursday because my birthday is on that day."

"No problem. How are things?"

"I'm trying to adjust."

"At first it can be a bit overwhelming."

"A bit? I don't believe that's the word to describe it."

He laughed and got up. "You'll get used to it."

We walked out of the restaurant, confirming business with a handshake.

"Thanks for everything, Scott," I said.

He tapped me on the shoulder. "Don't mention it."

* * *

That afternoon, I rode to get a haircut for the upcoming *Dime* magazine photo shoot. I held my chin up as Larry trimmed my goatee. My barber always kept me looking sharp. He loved to crack jokes on me too. "I remember when this boy used to come in here with ashy lips and knee caps. Now look at him," he said, spinning me in his chair. He had the whole barbershop rolling, including me.

I enjoyed coming back to the hood to see my peoples. There were a few of them that admired me for making it out of the gutter. Larry was one of them.

Floyd walked in the barbershop and sat down. He stared at me with an angry look on his face. I got up and handed Larry twenty-five dollars, never minding Floyd's evil stares.

Larry dug in his pockets for change.

"You better not hand me back no change," I said.

"I appreciate it, brother. It seems like just yesterday that you used to come in here begging for a haircut and now look at you. I'm proud of you."

"Thanks, Larry."

He smiled and gave me a strong pat on the back. "Take care."

When I walked out of the barbershop, I felt the tension. Floyd eyed me all the way to my truck. I didn't trust any of my old friends. My new best friend was nina.

* * *

I celebrated my 20th birthday at one of the hottest nightclubs on Miami Beach. A lot of big name stars of my draft class were in the building while beautiful women flocked through the doors. After a while, the doors had to be closed.

The club was rocking to "All I Do Is Win" by DJ KHALED. Brandon was at my side with a bottle of rosé shouting, "All I do is win win win no matter what!"

I had a glass of rum and Coke in hand while enjoying the scene. The women were bold. They completely disregarded Lindsey as she stood next to me. One girl grabbed me and shouted that she wanted to do me. Apparently, Lindsey didn't like it. She threw a drink in the girl's face. "Fucking, whore!" she shouted at her.

I grabbed Lindsey and held her back. "Chill, yo. All that isn't necessary," I said.

All night it was the same ordeal with women. If it weren't for Lindsey at my side, I probably would've lost my mind.

After the party, Lindsey gave me a big surprise. I almost crashed into the vehicle in front of me. "For real?" I said.

She smiled. "Yes."

I kissed her lips. "I love you."

This time around, I was ready to be a responsible father.

* * *

When I got back in town from New York, I felt on top of the world. The two-million-dollar deal with Under Armour had fallen through. That same night, I partied like a rock star at Cameo nightclub on South Beach. I threw away money on a caseload of expensive champagne for my section. Several groupies surrounded Brandon and I. Many of them could fit the cover of a *Cosmopolitan* magazine.

After partying the night away, Brandon and I ended up at the hotel with three drop-dead gorgeous women. There were no limitations to what they would do for us; we were in heaven, as they fulfilled our fantasies.

When I crept in the door at 5:00 a.m., Lindsey was sitting on the couch. "Where were you?" she said.

"Out with Brandon, why?"

"What do you mean, why? It's only five o'clock in the morning."

My phone rang.

Lindsey got up and snatched it away from me. She had lost her mind.

"Give me the phone!" I said.

"No," she said, racing towards the bedroom. It appeared that she was calling someone. "Hello, who the hell is this?" she said.

I snatched the phone from her ear and hung up. "What's wrong with you? What would make you invade my privacy? You need to chill!"

"Who is she?"

"Who is who?"

"The frigging whore who picked up the phone."

"I have no idea"

"Don't play games with me."

"Why do you care? You're the one I come home to every night."

She took off her engagement ring and threw it at me.

I picked up the ring off the floor. "Oh, it's like that, huh?"

"Screw you!" She reached on the dresser for the keys to her Benz.

"Lindsey, don't leave, please. How do you think moving back with your parents is gonna make me look? We gotta learn how to work things out."

"I've had it up to here with you. I fucking swear."

"You know I love you and there isn't anything I wouldn't do for you. Give me your hand, Lindsey."

She held out her hand.

"If you ever take this off again, it's over," I said, sliding the rock back on her finger. Then I wrapped her in my arms.

* * *

A couple of days later, I contacted a realtor to find us a home in L.A. We were sent a list of properties in Beverly Hills, West Hollywood, and Los Angeles. The following week, we flew out to California to check them out. Lindsey was bossy. I thought we should've leaned toward a less expensive home in Los Angeles, while she was sold on a 4.6-million-dollar crib in West Hollywood. I looked at the realtor. "I think this is the one. Can you talk them lower?"

He smiled. "Certainly. This home was originally priced at $5.2 million. The owner took a big loss but it doesn't hurt to give it a try, right?"

"Of course not," Lindsey said.

"We'll work the numbers."

We walked out of the place confident that our realtor would get us the best deal. Then we shopped in Beverly Hills. We received star treatment in every store we'd go. And when it was time to wine and dine, we were waited on hand and foot. At the restaurant, I pulled out my credit card to pay for our food but the owner refused to let me pay.

After we left the restaurant, we checked into the Montage Beverly Hills Hotel. We were shown great hospitality.

Money was power.

* * *

When we got to Miami, I flew back out to attend an Under Armour photo shoot in New York. Later that day, I made a scheduled appearance at the House of Hoops to promote Converse shoe brand. It was a big turnout. A lot of kids and their parents were on hand to meet me. It was cool.

After spending two busy days in New York, I headed back home. Angelina had been blowing up my phone. I finally gave in and picked up. She was crying over bills. She needed money to move into her own place. Even though things didn't work out between us, we still kept an open line of communication. "I'll see what I can do," I said, blazing the highway.

"Please, I really need your help."

"I said I'd see what I can do."

"I owe you for this and I can't wait to give it to you, pappy."

"Nah, I'm good. I don't want anything in return." I couldn't believe I heard myself say that, but I was officially a one-woman man.

I wired Angelina $800 through Western Union.

When I walked out, I bumped into one of the ministers at my church. "I haven't seen you in church lately. We miss you," he said.

"I've been busy."

"You aren't too busy to tithe are you?"

"No, sir."

He smiled. "Well, amen. I hope to see you in church this Sunday, and if you can't make it, send us a love offering so that God will continue to bless you."

"Yes, sir."

"Matter of fact if you have a check or a money order, I can accept it on behalf of the church, right now."

I gave without any qualms about it.

On the way home, I got a surprise call from Chance. We hadn't talked in ages. He was still adamant about getting money for his dog fighting business. This time around he needed $60,000. "You'll get yours. I put that on my life," he said.

I entertained the conversation for several minutes, but I wasn't interested in throwing away money on dogs. Fighting dogs never interested me. On top of that, I didn't want that crap to come back and haunt me. "I'm not feeling it," I said.

"Please, do it for me; I'm your boy," he begged.

"I can't take that risk."

He got mad. "You a pussy! That's why you can't even come back to your own block. Everybody knows that you're a sellout. That's why cats got money on your head right now."

"I'm supposed to be scared?"

"Don't be scared, just watch yo' back," he said, hanging up.

I laughed it off.

* * *

The following week, I made a trip to Orlando and spent a few days at Angelina's place. I was able to relax and get away from the drama. I had spent the whole two days in peace. I felt bad lying to Lindsey about my whereabouts but I needed to get away.

This morning, Angelina kissed me on her way out for work. She seemed disappointed that we didn't sleep together, but there was no attraction there for me. I ended up leaving before she got home. I had left money in her drawer because I knew she was struggling to make ends meet.

That afternoon, she called and thanked me.

"No problem. Don't make it a habit," I said, hanging up.

As I headed back home, I stopped through Winter Haven to visit Doug. He was serving time at Winter Haven Correctional Facility. I missed him. At times, I wondered how would he deal with the pressure if he were in my shoes.

When I saw him, my heart bled. Prison life had hardened his appearance. I almost felt guilty that I hadn't come to see him sooner.

Doug didn't seem fazed. He grabbed the telephone as if he was happy to see me. "What's up?"

"I came to see how you were doing, bro."

Doug and I talked for fifteen minutes. It didn't matter that we had lost time and connection; we were still down like four flat tires. "So what's really going on outside of the glitz and fame?" he said.

"Life's been crazy. A lot of brothers can't accept that I've made it, you know."

"That ain't gon' ever change, so get used to it. Money is the root of all evil. The good book said it."

"I thought money was supposed to simplify my problems, not multiply them."

"You can blame that on the gap between "the haves" and the "have-nots". Trust me, it's not gon' get better. The jails and prisons are fillin' up faster than you can blink. You just be careful out there, bruh. I have a new outlook on life since I've been locked up. Ain't nothing worth your freedom and these cats don't understand that until they're faced with life." Doug sounded grounded. Too bad it took prison to reform him.

"You sound positive," I said.

"I gotta be, and you do too. Don't let nobody make you feel guilty because you chose a better way out. Do your thing; I ain't mad atcha. Just send me some change from time to time."

"I love you, bro, and you know that if you ever need anything, you can depend on me."

"That's a bet."

"I'll be in touch," I said, tapping the glass window. Just then, a corrections officer came in and escorted Doug out of the visitor's room.

I got up and left, feeling all right.

* * *

As I drove back to Miami, I was stopped within the city limits. I hadn't broken any laws. An officer slowly approached my Range Rover.

"What's the problem?" I said.

"License and registration."

I handed him both. "Why did you pull me over? I was driving the speed limit."

"Your tint is too dark."

"Are you serious? You're the first officer to have a problem with it."

"I'm only doing my job. Step out of the vehicle."

"What?"

"Step out of the vehicle!"

I slowly opened the door and got out. The officer frisked me and then proceeded to search my vehicle. A second officer walked up and assisted the searching officer. They searched my truck, as if they expected to find drugs. One of them walked up and questioned me about the gun in my glove compartment. "Are you aware of Florida's gun laws?"

I was quiet because I knew they had me at their mercy.

"I'm speaking to you," he said.

"Look, Officer, I've been carrying a gun for protection. I was robbed on two separate occasions and –"

"I understand that but hear me out: When you take the law into your own hands, you're asking for trouble."

I was read my rights and handcuffed. I couldn't believe I was going through this again.

28

I was charged with the unlawful possession of a firearm. I was given a court date to appear and released on bail. This time around, I didn't care what critics wrote or said about me. I had developed thick skin because it was obvious that people wanted to break my spirit. It wasn't happening though. I took all the insults and negativity with a smile while I lived the good life. I bought me a black-on-black, two-door Bentley because I had the money to blow. When I rode around town, it made a lot of folks mad. Often times, I was a victim of unnecessary traffic stops and searches. It was as if the police couldn't accept the notion that a brother could have nice things without scheming. It was insane, but the cops were my least concern. The continuous threats I received from cats in the hood bothered me the most.

Two weeks after my arrest, I appeared before a judge; he was a tough one. I was charged with a misdemeanor, handed a $1000 fine, and sentenced to 14 days in jail. Those fourteen days in jail was tough. I hated being away from my family, but I did my time like a man. There wasn't a moment I didn't regret having that gun. I'd learned my lesson.

When I was released, I put everything behind me and remained strong. My family helped me get through it, especially Lindsey.

* * *

Mid-July, I left town for summer league in Vegas. I was happy to be back at it. When I arrived, it was a very competitive atmosphere filled with new rookies, undrafted free agents, and veterans that hoped to earn an invitation to training camp. I reunited with Mario. He had an unguaranteed contract with the Spurs, while Ricky had opted to play overseas after not getting drafted. I was blessed. And I was eager to make a strong debut considering I'd been passed over in the draft for other players. I didn't have any hard feelings though.

During our team's five-game schedule in Vegas, I made a statement to one of the participating teams that passed on me during the draft. I had 25 points, 6 assists, 9 rebounds, and 2 steals against the Houston Rockets. It was my NBA debut and I "delivered," like many sports analysts bragged.

On the third night in Vegas, Lindsey called me upset. She was frantic because someone had tried to break in, setting off the alarm. My fun night out with the homies had turned into a scary one. I stood outside the casino trying to gather information from Lindsey. I was told that she and a friend were in the kitchen when the alarm sounded.

"You sure it wasn't a false alarm? You know those sensors are sensitive," I said.

"No, but the police are here now, so we're fine."

"Don't hang up. I wanna hear what's going on."

"I won't."

I stood outside for forty-five minutes, ear pressed to the phone. I clearly heard the conversation that she had with one of the officers. This was one time I regretted being miles away. All I could think about was someone harming my family.

I spent the last two days in Vegas anxious to get back home. Basketball was my least concern as I rose above competition on the court.

* * *

When I touched ground in Miami, I felt relieved to be home. I got in my car and put the pedal to the metal. It was 1:30 a.m. and I was ready to get home to my bed.

As soon as I pulled into the garage, I fell asleep behind the wheel. I was too tired to move. Lindsey tapped on the window, waking me up. I grabbed my luggage and got out of the car. When I walked in the house, there were six people in the living room drinking, smoking, and having a good time. I saw a white powdery substance on the table and lost my cool. "Everybody get the fuck out!" I said.

Everyone looked startled and quickly hit the door. Lindsey looked embarrassed as I kicked her friends out. After everyone left, she barked at me. "What the hell is your problem?"

I pointed to the cocaine residue on the glass table. "That's my problem and if you have a problem with it, then you can hit the door too."

"I'm so sorry."

"I don't want that stuff around me and you should know better," I said.

"I swear I didn't know."

"That's okay, but due to circumstances, we need to limit company. Is that fair?"

She hugged me. "I understand."

"Good," I said, heading to bed.

* * *

The next morning, I woke up feeling good. I had a dream-come-true day ahead of me.

At noon, I met with a billionaire investor in regards to a restaurant venture. He wanted to partner in a sports bar/restaurant bearing my name. I was excited at the idea of owning a business.

Richard took me for a ride on his expensive yacht. It was a bright sunny afternoon. Most everybody took advantage of the nice summer weather. The sea was brimmed with boating activity while tourists crowded the beach to soak up the sun. Fort

Lauderdale Beach was beautiful. And so were the women on Richard's yacht. They lay baking in the sun topless, while I had on my shades, peering over the edge at all the beautiful mansions along the waterway. It was amazing. I felt like I was in paradise as I bobbed my head to Sade's "Kiss Of Life."

Richard brought me a glass of champagne and started talking business. I thought Parker's Place was a brilliant name for the spot. I agreed to partake in the business as part owner. He laid out the terms, and everything sounded good. After talk negotiation, Richard handed me a gift. I opened the box and it was a set of diamond cufflinks. He boasted that they were $80,000.

One of the ladies got up after sunbathing. She was topless and nicely toasted; her nipples were at full attention.

Richard smiled and nudged me. "Nice tits, eh?"

I nodded.

"She's *Playboy* Centerfold of the Month."

I perused her body but I wasn't impressed. "Um, okay."

"Have you ever been to the Playboy Mansion?"

"No."

"You don't know what you're missing, kid. Why don't you get acquainted with Ms. Claudia?" he said.

The toasted Playboy Bunny smiled at me.

"Nah, I'm good," I said.

"Come on, you only live once. You're young, good looking, and rich. Have a little fun."

"I'm cool." I liked beautiful women, but I was smart enough not to mix business with pleasure.

* * *

When I got back home, I dropped the good news on Lindsey. She was excited too. "I can't believe it!" she said.

I wrapped my arms around her body. "Believe it. Your man is on fire!" I said, pecking her on the lips.

Two hours later, Momma called and ruined the day with news that Grandpa had passed. I was hurt. After talking to Momma, I called my grandmother. She seemed fine because she had done all she could do. My grandmother asked me for the money to bury him. I jumped at the opportunity to help her because she'd never asked me for a penny.

* * *

A week later, Grandpa's funeral was held at a small church. My grandmother was strong. She held up, while my aunties and uncles nearly jumped in his casket.

After the funeral, everyone gathered at my grandmother's house for the repast. I fixed Lindsey a plate of food, although she was very particular about what she ate. I could barely eat because Uncle Gary was campaigning for me to invest in his idea of a home inspection business. I finally agreed to give him the money to start up the business. One of my cousins who I met for the first time pitched the idea of a clothing line to me. I agreed to help him, too, since he was trying to make moves.

Lindsey seemed bothered that everyone was harassing me for money.

I wrapped my arm around her shoulders. "Are you okay?"

"No."

"What's wrong?"

"I don't want to talk about it right now."

I stayed at her side for the rest of the evening. The moment she was ready to go, I got up. I gave everyone a hug before I walked out the door. Al though everyone was sad that Grandpa was gone, there was a sense of relief because he didn't have to suffer no more.

Momma waved goodbye as we headed to the car. I held the passenger's side door open for Lindsey. When I closed the door and looked over my shoulder, Chance was standing on his porch shaking his head.

"You and your white bitch need to stay outta Opa-Locka! Ol' fake ass, motherfucker!" he shouted.

I brushed off his comments and rode away in my Bentley.

* * *

The same week of the funeral, I rode to the bank to withdraw funds for my grandmother. She needed the money for Grandpa's tombstone. I hit I-95 with Drake on blast in my stereo. When I got to Opa-Locka, it was dreadful to see bums sleeping on the streets. While sitting in traffic, I recognized the bum that I'd met at the park a long time ago. He had a cardboard sign in his hand. A lot of people refused to let down their windows.

"'Ey, yo!" I shouted.

He ran over to my truck. "God bless you, brotha."

I handed him twenty dollars and he bolted away happy.

When I got to my grandmother's house, Tasha wouldn't let me get in the door without asking for money. She and her friends were in the front yard looking like hoochies. "Can I please borrow three hundred dollars, Cousin?"

"For what?"

"My birthday's coming up and I wanna throw a party."

"I'll think about it."

"Can I have it at your house?"

"Maybe, we'll see."

I walked in the house. My grandmother was sitting on the couch. I gave her a hug and then made myself at home. We talked for a while and then I headed on my way. When I walked outside, Tasha was hugged up on a nappy-headed boy. The boy had his hands on her butt.

"Yo, you need to ease up," I said.

The boy looked at me and backed away afraid. "That's your cousin for real?" he said, tapping Tasha on the sly.

"Duh, I told ya." She began to pressure me for three hundred dollars again.

"Won't you ask him, since he wants to touch and feel on your booty?" I said, pointing at her friend.

"I'm broke, dawg," the boy said.

"You better get a job."

"Ain't no jobs. We in a recession."

"Stop making excuses. I got a job for you," I said.

"For real?"

"Yeah, I'll hook you up." I had rather put a hundred dollars in his pocket instead of a lawn service. He seemed excited to do the work. It made me feel good to help a young brother out.

* * *

Over the past two weeks, I was on a roll doing a lot of positive things in the community. I attended Zo's Summer Groove and gave a big donation to charity. Spending a couple of days around the kids made me realize how much they looked up to a brother. It sent chills down my spine when I saw dozens of kids with my NBA jersey on their backs. The experience was unreal. Alonzo Mourning's big charity event inspired me. Brandon and I had planned on teaming up and holding a free basketball camp next year.

In the meantime, with the help of Lindsey and family, we established Parker's Foundation in order to give back to the community through outreach programs and donations. I thought the foundation could've thrived with exposure from the media, but they weren't interested in positive news. If a brother wasn't out getting arrested, they didn't care to cover the story. I didn't sweat it while I continued to give back to my community. It was a shame that I still didn't get any respect from my peers in Miami.

* * *

At the end of August, Lindsey and I closed on our new home in West Hollywood. We spent a couple of weeks in California getting used to the change of scenery. During that time, we furnished our new place and made it a home. I got acquainted with several of my new teammates and they showed me around the big city. Most of them had wives, and Lindsey clicked with them well. Some nights we would have get-togethers at each other's homes or go bowling. Other nights, me and the guys would hit the club. One thing that never changed was the women in nightclubs. They were the same in every city: desperate for an NBA star to rock their world. At times, it was a bit much to handle but Lindsey kept me grounded. I knew that I had something good at home regardless of what came my way.

One night, I lay in bed rubbing Lindsey's stomach. She was two months. I was happy that we were having a boy. There was no joy like having a son.

My phone rang while Lindsey and I discussed names for the baby; she wanted Justin, while I thought he should be named after me. I answered the phone. Momma told me that someone had broken into our home in Miami. I had an $80,000-pair of cuf-flinks in a safe located in my closet. Momma told me that the safe had been broken into and the intruder had left behind a crowbar on the bed. I was so upset that I couldn't think. I talked with an officer over the phone and reported everything I had in the safe.

After I got off the phone, Lindsey hounded me to death. I sat at the edge of the bed ready to fly off the hinges.

"Who do you think it could've been?" she said, leaning over my shoulder.

"How am I supposed to know? I swear on my daddy's grave if I catch the motherfucker I'm going to jail."

Lindsey crawled underneath the covers. "Will you come lay down?"

"I'm not sleepy."

I got up and went outside on the balcony for a while. Marijuana smoke filled my lungs. It still wasn't enough to take my mind off of things.

Lindsey peeped outside, looking half-asleep. "Jermaine, will you come inside?"

I acted as if I didn't hear her as I puffed smoke into the air.

"Please?" she begged.

I put out my joint and then went back inside. I lay in bed awake, unable to rest. It seemed as if I had everything in the world except for peace of mind.

* * *

When we got back to Miami, I felt like going on a rampage. I checked the perimeter of the house. Then I went inside to conduct my own investigation. Roy had used a piece of plywood to board the glass door.

White Chocolate pointed out the disconnected wires on the sensor of the door. "That's what you call a smooth criminal," he said.

My temper fluctuated. The thought of my girl being home during the break-in had me ready to jump off the deep end. Everything pointed to Floyd. "I've had enough of this shit, bro!" I said, storming out of the house.

White Chocolate followed me. "Where are you going?"

I hopped inside of my Chevy Camaro and revved up the engine.

White Chocolate stood in front of the car. "I know you're upset, but you really need to pause before you do something you may regret."

"Move outta the way, bro."

"Real talk, Jermaine. You stand way more to lose than a bunch of rats. I can't let you go out this way."

"I said move! Now move your ass out of the way!" I put the car in drive and rolled forward a few inches, touching him with the bumper.

"No! You can kick my ass or run me over but I'm not letting you leave here angry."

He made me re-think things. It only took a few seconds to have a change of heart, considering I couldn't afford to get into trouble. I got out of the car and White Chocolate held out his hand for the keys. "Are you serious?" I said.

"Yes, I'm serious."

I handed over the keys.

"Thank you," he said.

* * *

At night, I slept with a machete under my bed for protection. Every little noise heard throughout the house made Lindsey flinch, unlike me. I refused to live in fear.

One stormy night, the branches tapped against the window, making Lindsey squeal. Then she curled up behind me like a scene out of *Paranormal Activity*.

I looked over my shoulder at her. "Will you cut it out? It's only the wind."

"I don't like it here anymore. This house is too big for us."

"You weren't complaining about the size of it before."

"Well now I am. When we leave, I don't want to come back."

I turned over and we lay face to face. "What are you so afraid of? I'm not gonna let anything happen to you."

She loosened up.

"Thank you," I said. Then I turned back over, staring into the darkness. Although I feared no man, but God, I was ready to start my life over in a new city. The drama in Miami was getting old.

A week later, I received a call from the Miami Police Department saying they had recovered my property from a sixty-year-old jeweler who reported it stolen. The police arrested two black males. One of them was Tasha's boyfriend – the same cat I had doing yard work for me. I'd learned my lesson after that one: *I can't help everybody.*

29

LINDSEY AND I HAD A going-away party with family and friends. Then we officially made our move to California. The first two months was smooth sailing as we got used to life in a different city and traveled abroad. Over the summer, we spent a week in Paris, France. Lindsey went out of control on expensive shopping sprees but I didn't mind. When it came to what she wanted, my Black Card had no limit. Seeing her happy made me happy.

Lindsey led me into a bridal shop. I watched her squeeze into a $10,000 wedding gown. Although she was four months pregnant, it was hard to tell she was carrying a baby with her shape. "You like it?" she smiled.

"It's alright." I was getting impatient as she tried on more dresses.

She walked out of the dressing room. "What about this one?"

"I like it," I said.

"I do too, but it's twenty thousand dollars."

"On second thought, I don't like it. Go take it off."

"When is the wedding?" the salesperson asked us.

"We haven't set a date," Lindsey said.

"Next June."

Lindsey seemed surprised.

"Congratulations and I wish you two the best!"

"Thank you," I said.

Lindsey walked in the dressing room and changed. When she came back out, she sat on my lap and started kissing all over me while I was on a business call.

People were looking at us as she showed me affection. One woman covered her child's eyes when Lindsey stuck her tongue in my ear.

"Not in the store," I said, hanging up the phone.

"Then let's go."

We spent the rest of the week making love into the night as if we were already on a honeymoon.

* * *

Lindsey and I were happy in love until the season got underway. The pressure of stardom was beyond unimaginable. Late night partying and trust issues brought friction between us. I was living life out of control. It was hard to be a perfect man when everyone in my circle was abusing alcohol, drugs, and running through women. I had a lot of newfound friends. People were attracted to me for many reasons. I was spending money and taking care of a lot of people. The spotlight had celebrity women looking my way too. Every day I was battling temptation and losing the fight.

During preseason, I lived up to the hype, averaging 16.5 points, 7 assists and 9 rebounds per game. The media had me in conversation topics such as Rookie of the Year. Brands such as Icy Hot and Right Guard rode the wave, offering me major deals. Money was no object. I had plenty.

One night at a club in Miami, I bought the bar. People surrounded me like I was king. One of the Miami Heat dancers was all over me. She was a bright-skinned cutie pie with long hair. I couldn't keep my hands off her tiny waistline. As we danced, I felt someone bump into me. I looked behind me.

Floyd was in my face shouting, "You ain't nothin' but a snitch, nigga!"

I reached for the bottle of vodka sitting on the bar counter. I was a second away from busting him across the head. My bodyguard grabbed the lunatic and dragged him away, just in time.

"You better stay outta Miami, punk bitch!" Floyd shouted at the top of his lungs.

"Here I am! What are you saying, bro?" I shouted back.

My teammate shook his head. "What a fucking clown."

I shrugged off the incident. Then I pulled the cutie pie dancer back close to me.

"What the hell was his problem?" she asked me.

"I have haters, what can I say?"

Cutie started rubbing up against me with her bottom. She was making it bounce to "Hello Goodmorning" by Dirty Money. All night I had a great time watching her put it down.

When I got back in town from a two-game road trip, Lindsey jumped on my case. Our relationship was hurting. Tonight was the cream of the crop. Lindsey had been emailed photos of me at the club in Miami. The pictures had surfaced over the Internet. MediaTakeOut.com had put me on blast.

Lindsey lost her cool and shoved the computer to the floor. Then she came after me. "What do you have to say this time, you cheating bastard?" she said, shoving me.

"Don't put your hands on me." I walked away to avoid further drama.

"How dare you cheat on me with a frigging whore!"

When I didn't respond, she started swinging at me. She bloodied my lip after landing a punch to my face.

I grabbed her and squeezed her tightly in my arms. "Calm down!"

She kicked and screamed. "Take your hands off me!"

"No, not until you calm down. That girl doesn't mean anything to me. It was only a dance."

She ran out of strength in my arms. "Why are you doing this to me?"

I laid her down on the couch and gave her time alone. My conscience was killing me as she cried from the living room. I took off my suit and stared at the man in the mirror. He was out of control.

3 0

THE FIRST REGULAR SEASON GAME against the Lakers, I fell to the floor after turning my ankle on Odom's foot. I was in excruciating pain as I curled up on the hardwood floor, clutching my foot. My teammates surrounded me, urging me to get up but I couldn't.

The arena lost its pep for a minute.

Our team's trainer, Luke, ran out to the floor and assisted me. "Can you move it?" he said.

"No, I think it's broken." I was helped to the bench and the fans cheered for me. Luke worked on my foot. I grimaced in pain as he eased off my shoe.

"This doesn't look good," he said, touching the swollen flesh around my ankle.

I threw my towel to the floor upset. "Fuck!"

My teammates tried to console me. "Take it easy. It's gon' be all right," Randy said.

When I got up to head to the locker room, some of the fans looked worried. I happened to catch a few of their dejected faces on the way to the locker room. It was a scary walk down the tunnel, as I prepared to get looked at by the team doctor.

Luke helped me up on the table.

"Thank you," I said.

Lindsey came running through the door, looking deeply concerned. "Are you okay, baby?"

"Yeah, I'm okay."

She kissed me on the cheek while I dripped sweat all over the place. "What happened?"

"I hurt my foot."

The doctor gave me an X-ray and the results were heartbreaking. I had a fracture in the same foot I'd injured in high school. Surgery was a given.

I walked out the arena on crutches pondering my future. Doubt and fear consumed me. With a serious foot injury like this one, I didn't know if I could bounce back right away. I got in the car with Lindsey, feeling down and out. My cell phone rang nonstop. Everybody was seeking information. My mother and my agent were the only two people I let know the deal. Everyone else could go to hell considering they probably wanted to see me hit rock bottom.

* * *

I had surgery on my foot. Under doctor's orders, I had to rest. I spent a lot of time playing video games because there was nothing else to do. Every now and then I would get a surprise visit from my teammates whenever they had time. Other than that, I stayed cooped up in the house frustrated. I'd hit rock bottom. All the talk of my injury had me banging my head against the wall.

My injury had companies backpedaling. A lot of offers that I had on the table were put on hold and my phone no longer ringed. I learned the ugly side of the business quickly. All the people who I thought I had in my corner had bailed. It made me hard to be around at times. I figured that was the reason Lindsey stayed on the go with her friends. Her inner circle consisted of the wives and girlfriends of other NBA players. I couldn't stand it because they corrupted her mind. Lately she had spunk, making matters worse. The good girl I once knew had turned into a mess. The good book helped me cope with a lot of madness.

One day, I was sitting on the couch playing NBA Live like a madman. Lindsey started complaining of pain. I didn't pay her any mind because I had my own problems.

Later that night, she went into labor. I stood in the delivery room and watched Lindsey push out a baby. I cringed at the sight of her vagina being stretched the size of a large cantaloupe.

After she pushed out the baby, the nurse placed him in her arms. He was abnormally small. The doctor informed us that he'd have to be placed in an incubator for a period of time. It upset me.

I remained at the hospital all night. I wanted my son to be all right. I stared at him from a glass window with tears in my eyes. If it weren't for Momma, I probably would've lost it. Every hour on the hour, she would call to make sure that we were all right. For once in my life, money didn't matter or make a difference.

I hobbled down the hallway on crutches. When I walked in the room, Lindsey was asleep. As I sat in the room at her side, I promised God I'd be a better man if he brought my son home healthy.

* * *

Two weeks later, Justin Jermaine Parker came home. Momma flew out to California to help us with the baby. She and Lindsey got along very well. It was cool to watch them bond. My son had everybody happy. Having him home was a joy. He took my mind off a lot of crap even though I was pressing. I wanted to play and the injury to my foot didn't seem to be healing fast enough. I still had a lot of pain. At night, it bothered me the most. I'd pop pain-killers like it was candy.

One night, Lindsey watched me take my medication while she sat in bed breastfeeding. "Jermaine, you can't keep taking those painkillers in that manner."

"I'm hurting."

"Why don't you call your doctor?"

"He said it's normal."

"This is not normal. It's been three weeks. There's nothing normal about your condition."

"This is some freaking bullshit!"

"You should call and let me speak to him."

"No, stay in your lane."

"Hell no. Someone needs to get on his case."

I sighed. "I'm gonna get a second opinion."

After the Percocet kicked in, I was finally able to get some rest.

* * *

Two weeks passed and my ailing foot wasn't making any progress. The Clippers' organization was getting impatient and so were the fans. The fans ate me up on blogs, protesting that I was soft. They constantly wrote that the Clippers should've bypassed me in the draft due to the emergence of late second round picks. My close friend, Brandon, who played for the Cavs, was one of the emerging rookies mentioned. The media had formulated their opinion of me too. They considered me a softie and injury prone like Tracy McGrady. It hurt to read all the negative things written about me.

Momma walked through the door with groceries while I sat in the living room watching the local news. At the start of the sportscast, my injury was the topic of discussion. "I say the Clippers shop for a reliable point guard before the trading deadline," the sports announcer suggested.

Momma turned the channel. "Jermaine, stop watching that garbage. Where's my pumpkin pie?"

"In his crib sleeping."

"Where's missy?"

"I don't know."

"Let me guess, at the mall spending money like there's no tomorrow?"

I grabbed my crutches and got up.

"Where are you going?" she said.

"Nowhere." I went outside on the balcony.

Five minutes later, Momma came out to see about me. She stood beside me while I overlooked the city in misery. "Baby, look at me," she said.

I looked at my mother.

"You can't let anyone or anything break you. You hear me?" she said.

"I'm not but all this has taught me a lesson: everyone loves you when you're on top."

"Welcome back to the real world."

We saw Lindsey walk in the front room. She had shopping bags in hand.

"When's the wedding?" Momma said.

"June."

"Prenup!"

Lindsey waved at us.

After I waved back, I looked at my mother. "Please don't start. She's not even that type of girl."

Momma threw her hands in the air. "Okay."

I hobbled inside from the balcony, feeling extremely warm and nauseated.

Lindsey kissed me. "How are you, babe?" she said.

"Still in pain."

"Unbelievable."

The next morning, Lindsey raised hell at the doctor's office. It was apparent that something was wrong. After the doctor looked at me, he confirmed that I had an infection and that the fractured bones in my foot weren't healing properly. When he suggested a second surgery, I went ballistic.

"You've got to be kidding me!" I said.

"I'm sorry, Mr. Parker," he said.

31

LINDSEY, JUSTIN, AND MY NAGGING mother flew with me to Miami. I was cleared to see one of the best foot surgeons in Miami. A day before surgery, I sat home watching the gossip on my injury.

"I'm sure he will recover and come back from an injury like this and help the Clippers' organization get on the right track. Don't count this kid out."

"I don't know. I mean, what do we really know about this guy? Sure he's an impact player, but just how reliable is he should be the question. If you look at the overall picture, he didn't play a complete year of collegiate ball, missing games due to disciplinary action. I'm sure the owner is scratching his head on this one because when you draft high, you expect big returns on your investment and who's to say he isn't a bust?"

"Blah blah blah," I said. I turned off the television and grabbed my crutches. When I walked into the bedroom, Lindsey was watching "Jersey Shore" and Justin was in my spot. "Can you move him out of the way and turn off that stupid show?" Lately I couldn't take the presence of people in my space.

Lindsey turned down the TV and then grabbed our son out the way. She put him in his crib and then got back in bed.

I laid down and pulled the covers over my shoulder. All night, I lay in bed stressed out. In the middle of the night, I felt Lindsey's lips touch mine. I turned away because romance was the last thing on my mind.

"Are you okay?" she said.

"I'm fine."

"Face me."

I slowly turned over. We lay in bed face to face.

Lindsey grabbed my face and kissed me. "I know things seem uncertain, but don't push me away. It's time like this that makes me want to be the closest to you."

We started kissing and touching. I got on top and Lindsey squeezed me as if she was yearning for my loving.

Justin started whining.

"You little monster," I said, rolling over to my side of the bed.

Lindsey got up and laid him in bed between us. She gave him a breast and it shut him up. All we could hear was him sucking away. I rubbed the top of his head, thanking God for giving me a son. Suddenly, life didn't seem so bad.

32

I HAD CORRECTIVE FOOT SURGERY. The prognosis was 4 to 8 weeks to heal and 10 to 12 weeks of rehab. Over the past eight weeks, I was making progress. I was in good spirits.

The sixth week, I had the hard cast removed from my foot. Everybody was hopeful that I would be back in action within the next ten weeks. I couldn't wait to be back on the floor to help my team. I was tired of sitting on the bench in street clothes, looking GQ. Some nights, I'd forget about my foot, and hop out of my seat in reaction to the game.

One night, I stood in a grey Armani suit, hoping we could win or tie the game with 1.3 seconds left on the clock. On the side inbounds play, Blake cut along the baseline off the screen, and put up a floater over Zach. The arena went mad, and so did we. I had to catch myself from celebrating.

After tonight's win against the Memphis Grizzlies, I headed straight home to bed. A few of the guys on the team tried to pressure me into going clubbing, but I didn't give in this time. I preferred being home with my family.

My son giggled as I blew loud noises on his belly with my mouth. His laugh and smile was beautiful. I couldn't believe he was partly my creation. Our father-to-son moment made me realize that I had everything I needed right at home. I looked at his beautiful mother and it was confirmation.

A week later, I started rehabilitation. It seemed like a long process as I worked with a highly recommended physical therapist. Every day she had me working hard. I spent a lot of time inside a hyperbaric chamber in effort to speed up things. By the tenth week, I was doing regular activities like running, swimming, and playing ball. I felt like I was ready to go after the twelfth week. I was hitting jumpers and dunking on cats at the park. The pain that'd held me captive on the bench was nonexistent. I was excited once I learned that I only needed medical clearance from my doctor.

One weekend, I headed back to Miami to see the surgeon who had performed my operation. Lindsey didn't skip a beat. She was right at my side through it all. When my doctor gave me medical clearance, a smile spread across my face. I walked out of his office in good spirits because I could play in our next game against Portland.

* * *

After the office visit, I went to check on the progress of Parker's Place. We were only in town for a day and I wanted to see our investment. I was impressed. The place was huge and sat in the heart of South Beach. I was excited about its grand opening in a week.

Lindsey and I ate at our new restaurant. The food was excellent.

After I ate, I stood outside talking to Scott on the phone. "I definitely feel I'm ready to give it a go," I said.

He was ecstatic over the news that I'd be back in action. "We're back in business, baby!" he shouted in my ear.

I swear I felt like a cash cow.

When we got home, I tuned into ESPN. I ended up falling asleep on the couch in front of the TV. That was until Lindsey woke me up to get in bed. I got in bed, trying to avoid smashing my son. He was knocked out cold.

Lindsey moved him over and made extra room for me.

"Thank you. Did you set the alarm clock?" I said.

"No."

"Can you set it for 5:45 a.m.?"

She set the clock.

Then I called Momma to make sure she'd be able to drop us at the airport in the morning. She had it squared away.

When we hung up, I closed my eyes. I couldn't sleep because I was afraid of missing our flight. As I lay in bed, I thought over my life, like how far I had come from a poor inner-city kid to a man of destiny. I was proud of myself for making something of my life, while most of my friends got sidetracked. In my heart, I felt like I had achieved my dreams and I wanted this moment forever.

Late into the middle of the night, I heard a sound in the living room. "You heard that noise?" I whispered, grabbing my machete off the floor.

"Yes," Lindsey said.

The sound of footsteps seemed to get closer. Lindsey grabbed our son out of fear.

I got up and scrambled across the room to close the door. My heart was beating fast. When I pushed the door closed, two gunshots popped like a firecracker. One hit me in the chest, sending me to the floor. It felt like a ball of fire was brimming inside my chest.

I lay on the floor in shock.

After a short period of time, Lindsey got up and turned on the light. "Oh my God!" she shouted and cried. She grabbed the phone and called 911, pleading for help. At that point, I was floating in blood. My heart was racing while I lay on the floor, asking God why me.

Suddenly, everything became blurry.

"Please, hold on, baby!" Lindsey cried out to me.

I could hear her voice, but I couldn't see her face. Everything in sight had faded and there was total darkness around me. All of a sudden, it became a struggle to breathe. My chest felt tight and my wind was cut off. I started gasping and trembling. Then I felt the sensation of someone trying to breathe air into my lungs.

"No!" a voice cried, as they pressed on my chest until I couldn't feel any more pain.

EPILOGUE

PARAMEDICS ARRIVED TO A HORRIFIC scene. Jermaine lay uncon-
scious and bleeding out. Lindsey's hands and clothes were stained
with blood. She cried as paramedics moved in. Immediately, they
dropped to their knees and checked for a pulse. "He still has a
pulse, but he's in bad shape!" one of them shouted, cutting the
blood-soaked T-shirt from Jermaine's wounded chest.

An officer pulled Lindsey away from the gory sight. He led
her and the baby out of the house while paramedics battled to
save Jermaine's life. Unfortunately, they were losing the fight. The
massive amount of blood on the floor made it difficult for his heart
to pump.

"We're losing him!" the paramedic shouted, as she adminis-
tered aggressive resuscitation. During the procedure, the paramedics moved in haste to get him airlifted to the nearest trauma center.
At the same time, special agents moved through the cold night
in search of the shooter. Police lights lit the streets in abundance.
Every block within a one-mile radius of the house was barricaded
with a police unit.

Covered in a blanket, Lindsey sat in the back seat of a patrol
car giving detectives thorough information. As she relived the ter-
rifying moment, she began shaking.

Justin began to cry.

"Shhh, Daddy's going to be okay," she kept trying to tell herself in the process. Her trembling hands managed to dial Janice. It was the hardest thing she'd ever had to do in her life. After Lindsey relayed the news, Janice arrived faster than the speed of light.

Janice hopped out of Roy's moving vehicle. Pushing her way past authorities, she ducked a string of tape and bolted onto the property.

"Miss, you're trespassing!" an officer yelled as she escaped his strong hold.

Janice reached the driveway. A sharp pain pierced her chest as she witnessed her son being loaded into an air rescue helicopter.

"Miss, are you okay?" another officer said, watching her fall to the ground.

Roy tried to pick her up but it was impossible.

"Oh, God, not my baby!" Janice shouted in disbelief. She began hyperventilating.

"Ma'am, please calm down and breathe," the officer said.

As air rescue ascended, Janice fainted.

Clinging to life, Jermaine arrived at Jackson Memorial in the nick of time. A doctor and a team of nurses moved hastily to save his life. As he lay on an operating table fighting, his chest was cut open to remove a .45 caliber bullet. The medical team had succeeded, but the severe loss of blood left Jermaine in a coma.

After two hours in surgery, he lay in intensive care. Family and friends had flocked to the hospital, crying and praying. Janice and Lindsey remained at Jermaine's bedside all night long. Neither of them had closed their weeping eyes.

When morning came, reports of the shooting flooded the news. Everyone in the world of sports was shocked. Fans who adored Jermaine were hurt. While people mourned a fallen star, the media painted the picture of a troubled man. Janice didn't take it well. During the doctor's press conference, she held up to defend her son. She dried the tears away from her swollen eyes and looked into the cameras. "Everybody, please pray for my son. He's always opened his heart to help others in need. He's not a bad person like people make him out to be ..." She began to weep uncontrollably. A group of family members embraced her and led her away from the podium.

* * *

A day later, police detained two suspects in connection to the burglary: Floyd Robinson and Luther Gay. While they remained in custody, detectives searched for two other individuals believed to be involved. As the hunt took place, detectives badgered Floyd and Luther.

"Who fired the weapon, goddamnit?" Detective Jackson said, pounding a fist on the table.

Floyd folded his arms, showing no sign of remorse. "I don't know."

"I'm going to ask you one more time, who fired the gun?"

"I told you I don't fucking know. Now get outta my face, nigga. I know my rights under the Constitution."

Detective Jackson fought hard to keep himself under control. If there weren't any consequences to bear, he would've strangled the piece of trash to death. "Whether you fess up or not, both of you bastards are looking at the same gun charges."

After antagonizing Floyd for two hours, Detective Jackson walked out of the room to take a break. It was a hard case for him to handle. Everyone was deeply affected over the senseless crime. Detective Jackson was approached by a fellow detective working the case.

"I got a confession out of Mr. Gay," Detective Reeves said.

Detective Jackson smiled as if he'd struck gold. "Yes!" he said.

Days later, the confession of Luther Gay had led to the arrest of 18-year-old Damien Crooks and 22-year-old Trevon Carter. During the interrogation, Damien broke down as he contemplated serving life inside a penitentiary. Detective Jackson had scared him into confessing. He admitted to breaking into Jermaine's home with three of his friends.

"What was your motive?" Detective Jackson said.

"I thought it was money in the house. I didn't think we were gon' shoot anybody," he said, crying a river.

"Where's the gun?"

"We tossed it in the Everglades."

Detective Jackson knew there was no hope of retrieving it. "Listen, who fired the gun, young man? You're doing well."

Damien sniffled. "Floyd."

"Thank you for your cooperation."

* * *

For a second straight day, Jermaine clung to life in ICU. Janice and Lindsey were hopeful that he'd come out of a coma. Over the past two days, he had shown signs of progress. He'd squeezed Lindsey and the doctor's hand on two separate occasions. The news was a delight to everyone pulling for him.

One afternoon, Jermaine's head coach and the GM made a visit to Jackson Memorial Hospital. Business had been set aside in the wake of the tragedy. Janice was touched as they extended their deepest sorrows.

"Jermaine is a great kid. We love him and he will always be a part of our family," the GM said, embracing her in his arms.

Teary-eyed, Janice looked at him and forced herself to smile. "Thank you," she said.

After close family and friends had spent the day at the hospital, Janice sat at Jermaine's bedside during the night. She watched her son, hoping he'd respond to her voice, like he'd done with Lindsey and his doctor. "I love you, Jermaine. Justin loves you, Grandma loves you, everybody loves you," she said, holding his hand.

Jermaine squeezed his mother's hand on his last breath, as if to say I love you and goodbye.

Clary Ingram would like to hear from you!
You may contact this author at:
writeclaryingram@gmail.com